Tomás González

Fog at Noon

Translated from the Spanish by Andrea Rosenberg

archipelago books

Library of Congress Cataloging-in-Publication Data available upon request.
ISBN: 9781953861887

Archipelago Books
232 3rd Street #A111
Brooklyn, NY 11215
www.archipelagobooks.org

Distributed by Penguin Random House
www.penguinrandomhouse.com

Cover photo copyright © Sebastião Salgado
Book design by Zoe Guttenplan

Epigraph from: César Vallejo's *Complete Poetry: A Bilingual Edition*,
trans. Clayton Eshleman, University of California Press, 2007

And Citation later (page 47): *Fernando Pessoa & Co: Selected Poems*,
translated by Richard Zenith, New York: Grove Press, 1998

This work is made possible by the New York State Council on the Arts
with the support of the Office of the Governor and the New York State
Legislature. This publication was made possible with support from the Hawthornden
Foundation, the Carl Lesnor Family Foundation, the National Endowment for
the Arts, and the New York City Department of Cultural Affairs.

PRINTED IN THE UNITED STATES

Lo horrible, lo suntuario, lo lentísimo,
lo augusto, lo infructuoso,
lo aciago, lo crispante, lo mojado, lo fatal,
lo todo, lo purísimo, lo lóbrego,
lo acerbo, lo satánico, lo táctil, lo profundo . . .

The horrible, the sumptuous, the slowest,
the august, the fruitless,
the ominous, the convulsive, the wet, the fatal,
the whole, the purest, the lugubrious,
the bitter, the satanic, the tactile, the profound . . .
                              —César Vallejo (trans. Clayton Eshleman)

Fog at Noon

Raúl

The mountain where Raúl's and Julia's ranches are located is ever-changing. The climate is chilly rather than mild, and it's perpetually damp. Throughout the day, periods of rain, fog, and sun follow one after the other. Julia bought hers a long time ago, drawn by the area's lush vegetation, she said, and by the beauty of those rains and suns. He bought his just four years back, drawn by her. They got married in a picturesque colonial town three hours from Bogotá, and after two and a half years Julia left him, married another man in that same town some time later, and, seven months ago now, disappeared without a trace.

The vegetation is lush there because water abounds. Those who warn of a desertifying world have never visited those parts. There, the world will end in water. It falls everywhere, wells up everywhere, floats. Washed-out roads and mudslides are the biggest concern. Raúl's third of a hectare contains three springs; a stream known as El Raizal, which rushes noisily past about ten meters from the house; and, some thousand meters away, tumbling over large boulders down the mountainside, the Lapas River, which has been torrential of late. Winter—the rainy season—is hard going everywhere, but especially in this region, which is already so wet. Over the past three months, there's been as much rain here as usually falls in an entire year.

Sun, not so much.

Sitting out on the porch, Raúl is listening to the stream and the downpour and the river all in a chorus. His chair is made of cowhide with a very straight back. To avoid the tedious labor of building the wrap-around porch out of bamboo, he instead has installed a railing made of macana palm wood and a ceiling paneled with interlaced bamboo, each stem two centimeters in diameter. Raúl likes what he does. He never studied architecture; he learned from foremen and books and by keeping his eyes open. He graduated with an engineering degree a million years ago, worked in the field for two years, and got bored. He learned to work with bamboo and knows how to use it in his constructions without ruining the view. *Bambusa guadua*. Books about his work are published in sumptuous coffee-table editions, with spectacular photos and drab texts that nobody reads. Julia wrote four poems for one of them, and Raúl found them just as drab as the texts but told her he liked them. And since she was fairly renowned herself, the editors agreed to include them in the volume—or maybe they actually liked them.

Plenty of people admired her poems. The intellectuals who awarded her the occasional prize deemed them good, of course. Sometimes Raúl goes back and rereads them, trying to understand what everybody saw in them, but García Lorca's gypsy ballads are more his speed, and César Vallejo's poems, especially the two or three you can actually make any sense of. He hasn't read much poetry beyond that and doesn't consider himself qualified to pass judgments on the subject. When he told Julia how he felt about García Lorca, she'd said, "Only a shit-for-brains could find *Poet in New York* dull," and Raúl went ballistic. Afterward, Julia was always talking about his rages this and his rages that. She came to see him as an angry man.

As far as money goes, Raúl has neither too much nor too little, and he isn't stingy when it comes to investing in his property, which he keeps meticulously maintained. The pickup he uses to haul supplies isn't new, but it runs well. He doesn't regret selling the ranch he used to own near Cucununá, which was lovely but very dry, to buy this one. He's rented out the Bogotá apartment where he lived and worked for so long, and that serves as another source of income. He'd stopped using it after a while, preferring to stay "holed up on his ranch," as his friends say and as Julia used to say, accusing him of being a recluse. If Raúl ever went to Bogotá, it was for her and her alone. Recluses spend their lives within the hundred-square-meter confines of an apartment, Raúl thinks, or the fifty square centimeters of a car seat, yet it's him, the one who spends much of his day with no roof but clouds above his head, who's supposedly the shut-in. His business has one full-time employee, him, and a manager, him. He designed the logo—bamboo sprouting out of the soil like a huge asparagus—and painted it himself.

People invite him to come more than he wants to go, ringing him from all over the country. He also gives lectures on bamboo, and he's even traveled to Japan. He prefers designing whole houses rather than specific elements, though that has its charms too—ceilings, for example, almost always with a combination of *Guadua* bamboo and reeds, which look great together if you know what you're doing. He charges a bundle to ensure that people don't bother him much. He prefers blue-leafed reeds, which have thicker, shinier stems than regular reeds, which are slender with a strawlike texture that works well in folding screens and room dividers. He also uses papyrus, rushes, and palm fronds. When he gets to thinking about rushes and bamboos and reeds, the hours fly by as he contemplates possible combinations of textures and colors. Colombia is a paradise in terms of materials. Right by the turnoff to Bogotá, there's a group of artisans who weave dried banana bark to make wicker furniture. The pieces are a little rustic, but the texture has its appeal. Raúl is planning to go by the workshop this week to speak with them.

It was this infatuation with his work—"infatuation" was his sister Raquel's term—that saved him when Julia left him. Raquel hated her so much by the end! Raúl is still her baby brother, even though he's in his fifties and she's only got two years on him. If it hadn't been for his work, Raúl would have wasted away, or gone mad. He looked a fright.

Julia

I married five times, and every time I came out of it free and independent and unburdened by a husband complicating my life. No, six. I was never anybody's shadow. The locals used to say that when I got tired of my husbands, I threw them in the lake with rocks tied to their feet—how ironic—or buried them in the coffee grove, or went out and sold them. Well, that's what they said about the first four, who, unlike Raúl, went away and never came back. Jorge, the father of my two girls, died of leukemia, and Marcelo bled out in the hands of negligent paramedics after a car accident. I used to talk to the other two on the phone from time to time, or meet up for coffee in Bogotá if I happened to run into them. If a while went by without hearing from them, I'd call to find out how they were doing. But they couldn't claim I'd buried Raúl in the coffee grove because they used to see him on his ranch, which became increasingly overgrown—I obviously hadn't sold him off yet, ha. He put all his energy into his bamboo and his other obsessions, and grew more retiring and antisocial than ever.

Since I got a late start in my writing career—after I split up with my first husband—I had to give it my all, and I had no patience for people like Raúl, who demand too much attention with their quirks and obsessions. I love the beauty of simplicity. People probably say I was intolerant, but nothing could be further from the truth. I was more tolerant with him than with any of the others, because Raúl is an extraordinary person—I'm the first to acknowledge it—an artist in his own way, and I was actually really worried when I broke things off with him because I knew how much he loved me and I wasn't sure he could bear it. When I told him we needed to end it, that my love for him had died, I wrote a poem on my blog where I said that a person isn't in command of their own heart and that emotions should flow like rainwater, never standing stagnant. I wept as I had few times before. The poem was included in an anthology of Latin American women poets published in Buenos Aires at the end of that year. People appreciated it for the depth of its sensitivity and for my boldness in expressing what I was experiencing, without pussyfooting or hypocrisy. My poems touched my readers' souls. I was uncensored.

People who read or heard them were moved; they felt something of themselves or of the world through my words, and something magical happened. Something unpredictable and powerful.

Rain is so beautiful! It was incredible the way it hammered down on everything. I wrote a poem about precisely that, and there was this metaphor about it drumming on the banana leaves on Raúl's ranch and about the water flowing to join the larger current of the Lapas River, which never ever stopped noisily rushing.

"Hey, where's the off switch for that thing so we can get some sleep?" Humberto Fajardo asked me the first time he visited. The guy was a real jokester—who would have guessed he'd turn out to be so violent? And a total city slicker. He was astonished to see so much water everywhere, like in that poem I wrote about trees, how they look like jellyfish. How from my terrace, the mountains looked like the sea. They *were* the sea. Humberto liked my poems a lot, even if he didn't really understand them, because the waters I plied were deep and elemental. Above all, I am a lyrical person, a poet. He's into marketing—business, in other words—and extreme sports.

This place where I am now is like a hammock. So much peace. Lovely.

Raúl

Raúl's bamboo plants are for looking at—he never cuts them. At a lumberyard in Bogotá he buys bamboo from Quindío, already treated for termites, the Castilla biotype, larger in diameter than the varieties that grow in this region. He built columns using the fattest ones, which are nearly thirty centimeters in diameter and strong enough to hold up the Chrysler Building. He also buys reeds and rushes so he doesn't have to harvest his own. He created a grove of bamboo with a clearing in the middle where he placed two large, lichen-covered boulders that had to be brought in with a backhoe; they later became overgrown with ferns, some of them tiny and absolutely perfect. When it comes to ferns, they're either perfect or absolutely perfect. Regular bamboo forests are kind of pansy compared to the local ones, Raúl thinks. Though he does like the carpet of leaves they form. "More coals for Newcastle, eh,

Don Raúl?" the truck drivers tease when they show up to deliver supplies.

It's stopped raining. When that happens the fog creeps in, as it's doing now, and, without asking permission, slips into the house and leaves the furniture dripping. Or the sun comes out. Or there's fog and rain on one part of the mountain and sunshine and rain on another.

Raúl works because he enjoys it. True wealth, he thinks, is not needing much. Julia always insinuated that was false modesty on his part, a cliché, only a pretense of humility or even saintliness—in other words, hypocrisy. Raúl recalls the emerald dealer who offered him a ton of money to design him a house in the village of Pacho, near the Muzo mines. He was short and stout, very affable, and he had no neck. "Everything, absolutely everything of bamboo," the emerald dealer effused. Floors, walls, doors, stairs, railings, balconies, downspouts, gutters all made of bamboo. The stove and toilet would be the only things made of another material—though, with some effort, those could be bamboo too. The whole idea was a nightmare, so Raúl resisted any temptation to go after the money and turned down the job. The man was nice about it. He loved bamboo even more than Raúl did.

They offer him what he doesn't want to build; they tear down what he has built. He'd been so fond of the little chapel he erected in a town in Caldas, the most beautiful thing he'd ever made. Seeking to finally purge his grief over Julia, he'd poured his soul into it. Yes, they'd warned him the chapel would be temporary while the real church was being built, but a person doesn't build things thinking they're going to be torn down, so he hadn't asked what they meant by temporary. Bamboo arches and semiarches, walls made of mud and rush mats, sometimes exposed, sometimes plastered with mud and horse dung and painted ochre and colonial red. Palm thatch roof. The pulpit was made of wattle and daub, also painted colonial red, and above it Raúl placed a simple cross made of macana palm wood, thick and practically black. Great richness in the parts and simplicity in the whole. You might almost think Raúl believed in God. Beautiful. Then the first thing a new parish priest did was tear it down, because we are not ants, he said, and should not build the house of the Lord out of manure and garbage. They were already holding mass in the new eyesore, full of hideous concrete columns and spikes, while the church was being built; it remained hideous even after it was finished. Temporary means temporary, the priest told him. Photos were all that was left of it.

Stupid priests.

Raquel

Raquel never understood how Raúl could have been so in love with such a ninny. He even lost his sense of humor—Raúl, who could be so funny sometimes. And she isn't saying this because he's her brother, though that does figure in too, since otherwise she'd never have even known the woman existed. She's mentioning it because that's how it was—she isn't making any of it up. And don't come at her with that whole song and dance about how the days of machismo are over and Julia wasn't obligated to be anybody's submissive wife, because it's not about that. Don't come at her with feminism. Raquel has been around feminists her whole life, so much so that they're starting to get on her nerves. She left him because she got tired of him; she left him because he didn't pay enough attention to her so-called career and didn't fawn over her every word and deed.

People who live for adulation, men and women alike, are vampires.

Yesterday afternoon was one of the biggest snowstorms Raquel's ever seen, and today the temperature plunged so low the Hudson froze almost all the way to the middle of the river. The ice is as blue as the salt cathedral in Zipaquirá. Ducks waddle across it. Raúl came to spend Christmas with her and Julián, and left just a few days ago. If he'd stayed another week he would have gotten to see the whole shebang, but eventually he was itching to get back— he must really miss that wilderness of his and his current girl.

He looked great! "You even gained back your chub," Raquel told him. But the girlfriend's too young to stay holed up on remote acreage with a fifty-something. She doesn't think it will last. It's not ugly, Raúl's land, those foggy mountains. Not that Raquel would live there herself. After thirty years in Inwood she'd go nuts with all that suffocating foliage. She belongs here now—sad. Or no, why sad? Reality's no better there than it is here. Not even in Phoenix! And there's the snow again, falling thickly past the window. Right out of a postcard. Very pretty until it starts turning black on the sidewalks, melting, getting gross.

When Julia left him, Raúl had stayed on his ranch for several weeks, engulfed in sadness. Concerned something might happen to

15

him, Raquel had invited him up, and after a lot of pleading, Raúl finally acceded and stayed with her and Julián for almost a month. So hangdog! Not even Julián, whose jokes had always made him laugh, could cheer him up. Raúl had shown up in August that time, during one of those summers that set everyone in the city gasping like catfish. Unable to sit still, he would go out for a walk at five in the morning and wouldn't come back till nine or ten at night. His sneakers stank like a corpse when he took them off, from all the sweat. He doesn't drink when he's having a hard time, he goes out walking, Raquel learned then. "I'll get you a basin of Clorox so you can rest your feet, you must be bushed," she'd say, and reluctantly he'd smile. "Don't worry too much about it, Raúl. Being pussy-whipped wears off eventually. It always, always, *always* wears off."

And it was at that point she told him she didn't get how he could have been so in love with that old dingbat.

It wasn't an insult—it was a description. Julia was no "spring chicken," as they said so elegantly here, and in Raquel's view the woman was a raving fool, despite her posturing and her renown and the appearances she kept up. Shame what happened to her, but let's call a spade a spade. Raquel has read her Emilys, her Gabrielas, her Sylvia Plaths, people who were actually good; she knows all about that, lives that, teaches that. She wasn't fooled. The poems

16

seemed wise at first, but then you looked at them closely and looked again and in the end you could never figure out what the hell they were saying. And when you did figure something out, it would turn out to be a cliché. Plus, they were almost always about herself: *Me, profound blahblahblah, me me / Me, blahblahblah, me / Me, me, profound so profound, me, me / Me.*

Julia

My poetry was delicate and also complex, like the irises that bloomed around the borders of the flagstone patio at my ranch. Pubis flower, Humberto Fajardo jokingly called it. The last time I saw them, the irises were swathed in a thick midday fog. I nearly wept. When the fog came up to my house, it was like everything was floating on the clouds. Or floating *with* the clouds. I would study the verbal possibilities of an idea and then the poem would pour out. My poems grew that way. I never pressured a poem or forced it, and they always touched people deeply. As did my singing, which I studied for many years. That doesn't mean a person shouldn't write a lot or should hold back if they're prolific, as I was. One thing doesn't cancel the other out. Almost like how the waters were born and reborn: perennial and ever pure.

There's a little echo right there between "perennial" and "pure."

Prolific and rebellious. A nonconformist. And it wasn't my success—relative success, of course, as it always is—that they wouldn't forgive me for, but the fact that I'd accomplished things the way men do. No unassuming little girl, no way. No writing little books on the off-chance somebody might notice them. In this arena you have to launch yourself forward, push them, promote them. Write your own reviews if necessary, and you weren't deceiving anybody, because you believed what you were saying, you believed in what you were promoting, in yourself. That's what Walt Whitman did. Wily old Walt Whitman! Making sure his name appeared in the papers. If I'd been a novelist, my agent would have taken care of that, but poetry doesn't work that way. It is the oldest form of literature and the one that sells the least. Things used to be different; poetry was king, not the market.

Aleja

Aleja thinks Raúl was far too basic a man for a woman like Julia. She never said so, of course, even though they were best friends, because a person shouldn't meddle in such things . . . Not basic. That's not the word at all. *Straightforward.* Too straightforward, she thinks, for someone who was so vulnerable about her work, her passion, her life.

Raúl never understood that Julia, a sensitive woman, might have reacted so harshly, with such finality, only as a defense mechanism against his way of saying things. Or of saying them without actually saying them, which is often his style. When Julia left him, Raúl called Aleja several times to see if she could explain what had happened. No easy task. She told him that, as she understood it, he had handled the business of Julia's book badly, not because of what he'd said but because of how he'd said it. Raúl replied that there was only one way to say that an orange is sweet or that it's sour. "I think it's more humiliating for people to sugarcoat things like you're an imbecile." He was seething, about to fly into a rage. Aleja calmed him as best she could, since he was shattered, but she made no further attempts to explain her view of what had happened.

How can a person be so quiet and so plainspoken at the same time?

Based on physical appearance alone they were a mismatched couple. She is petite and vivacious, while Raúl is very tall, slow to move and slow to say the little he says. He's good-looking, sure, in his own way, despite the extra kilos, with that lovely skin color, like a Hindu, and those large, shiny eyes of his. Aleja thinks he liked her, since he was always affectionate toward her. Aleja is forty-five, and that's exactly how old she always claims to be, since nothing ages you more than pretending to be young.

As a yogi, Aleja believes in destiny and thinks the two of them were fated to go through this awful experience in their cycles of birth, life, death, and reincarnation. Obviously she didn't tell Raúl that. What for? Sure, they'd crossed paths there, he and Julia, both invited by the same university, but each of them doing their own thing. Raúl had already been living in New York for a year—he knew the city and offered to show her around. Here in Bogotá they might never have met. They moved in different circles. He spent his time out on his land, just like he does now, and she was busy with her readings and other poetry affairs. She'd been single for three years, ever since Diego. How can a person be a photographer with just one eye? Diego was missing his right eye and had a glass one in its place. Even so, he was handsome too, and more sophisticated than Raúl.

If she were him, Aleja would have worn an eyepatch.

Raúl

They first slept together in his apartment next to the Brooklyn Botanic Garden, in the depths of winter, February, and didn't come out for four days. The crows cawed in the gardens as the two of them drifted from sleep to love to sleep. This was three months before the return to Colombia. She was small and slight, but intense; she pervaded everything, while Raúl lay sprawled there faceup, motionless, in paradise. The images collected over the course of the two and a half years they were together still make him sad. Not too sad, though, since he paid a steep price for every single one of those trysts. If I'd known what was coming, I would have jacked off instead, he thinks. He'll have to tell Raquel that one; it'll make her laugh, since she's so crude.

Raquel couldn't stand Julia from the start. She didn't say anything to him that day, but Raúl could tell she wasn't a fan.

That odd way Julia had of going all childlike and talking like a ten-year-old girl, acting sweet and trying to ingratiate herself, raised Raquel's suspicions and eventually her hackles. He didn't like it much either, to be honest, but he gradually got used to it. One minute she'd be the sensitive poet, mature, profound, prepared to do anything for her career, and then suddenly, boom, here comes the little girl. Her father spoiled her, indulged her too much, however well-intentioned, Raúl thinks, and her mother hated and despised her. Her mother had been a trifling harpy when he met her, old and ugly, but she must have been a terrifying figure for Julia, and she had probably even been beautiful in her day. She used to give her daughter the silent treatment for weeks, as punishment. To a six or seven-year-old girl. Between the coddling and the contempt, that pair messed her up good. Those days in the apartment by the Botanic Garden were beautiful—they were in love, or at least he was—and that alone justified what he had to endure later on. Or almost. Who's to say.

Aleja

She's got to get the yoga academy in La Soledad on firm footing before opening the one in Santa Bárbara. Way north on Carrera Tercera or Carrera Cuarta. Crucially, Diana, Julia's eldest, has agreed to help her run the place and be an instructor. Four p.m. The day's flying by. An excellent yoga instructor and administrator, even though she studied design, completely unrelated. She'll be the perfect person to manage this place while Aleja gets the other one up and running. She's like a daughter to her. And may God forgive her, but Aleja thinks not having Julia around has been good for both of them, especially Diana. She doesn't have to keep proving how efficient and wonderful she is all the time, which made her snippy, just like it did her mom—they're a lot alike, actually, except Diana is tall like her father. And Manuela, who's just the opposite, really dependent, is much more her own person now.

Julia used to coddle them, fawn over them, but since she was so talented, she also overwhelmed them. Aleja knew that Diana had even hated her mother sometimes. One night the pair had gotten into an argument at Julia's apartment that ended in yelling and nearly in physical violence. When Aleja arrived, she could hear Diana's insults—crude and cutting—all the way down in the street, and when she walked in, a tense, sad silence fell that was soon shattered when Diana stormed out, slamming the door behind her. Aleja never learned what the fight was about, since neither of them said and she didn't want to ask. Diana didn't talk to Julia for almost three months, and during that time, whenever she mentioned her, she called her "that fucking poet." Then, following Aleja's advice, she made the effort to put herself in her mother's shoes and accept her as she was, as much as possible. They reconciled, and their relationship improved substantially after that. "My daughter's had a hard row to hoe, Aleja," Julia told her one day. "I wasn't the easiest mother." She was talented and ambitious, it's true, had been ever since they were in school together, but she could be a difficult friend. She sang like an angel, with a raspy, powerful voice that came from deep inside her. Diana stood up for herself better, but Manuela, maybe because she was younger and shadowed her mother's every move, absolutely revered her. Aleja isn't saying a little girl shouldn't revere her mom, especially in this case, but not to the point where she starts denying herself, either. It didn't come off that way, however. Manuela tried to assert herself, to act self-assured, but she always seemed anxious when she didn't have her mother to lean on. And without Julia around, she ended up getting into a relationship with a young man who was a good guy, sure, but very sexist, very basic. Now she runs the risk of becoming his shadow too, and though he claims he loves her, Aleja isn't so sure. She'll do everything in her power to break them up and help Manuela find a boyfriend who truly deserves her. Somebody more sophisticated, with more of a spiritual bent, since Manuela is very gentle—nobody would say otherwise, really almost treacly sometimes—but she's smart. She could also work with Aleja after she finishes university. Excellent grades. Two years go by in a flash. And besides, psychology is more closely related to yoga than to design.

The homeless guy who comes by several times a week to dig in the garbage bins just tore open the black bags in front of the yoga academy and is mercilessly scattering the contents all over the street. He doesn't care that it's pouring down rain or that she's watching him from the window. Aleja doesn't gesticulate for him to stop, afraid he might pull out his awful penis and show it to her. He'd done that before. Makes you want to vomit. Yoga teaches self-control. It always goes the same way. The cleaning woman sets out the trash all tidy and then that filthy animal shows up, rips the bags open, and leaves everything a total pigsty. Plus yells at you. They're thugs disguised as beggars, and now Katerina will have to go out and clean it up, poopy diapers, tampons . . . Poor thing, always in that immaculate white apron. Once it clears up she'll go out; no reason to get sopping wet out there now.

Raúl

Kissing in the aisles of Rite-Aid like teenagers. Photos among the flowering cherry trees in the Botanic Garden where he was doing his internship. April. A person is never too old for love and its absurdities, he thinks, nor for internships. Walking down the street, Julia would abruptly burst into song. Gorgeous voice— people used to compliment her. She should have dedicated her life to that instead, and Raúl would have been better off. He found himself deeply moved that afternoon as she sat in a pew in the middle of the Cathedral of Saint John the Divine and started singing *Ave Maria*. And a person is never too old for the numbing pain of a love that has been stabbed and left for dead. People have been drawing comparisons to hearts with daggers through them as long as there have been hearts and daggers and fucked-up women,

Raúl thinks, but when they leave you this way, it feels more like suffocation.

The cherry trees in the Brooklyn Botanic Garden are one of the world's minor wonders, surpassed as a minor wonder only by the dense bamboo groves of Quindío. Everything was beautiful; everything seemed auspicious, in the words of the *I Ching*, which Julia consulted often. They changed her ticket so they could travel to Bogotá together, and they kissed at the gate in Newark, kissed and groped each other on the plane, kissed in the passport line in Bogotá, long and slow, with five international flights that had arrived all at the same time as the weary, bored travelers stared listlessly at them, two people now getting on in years. They pressed up against each other, then dragged their suitcases forward a little bit before kissing and pressing again. They had spent the last three months kissing and pressing against each other in public and in private.

Love—beautiful on the inside and repellant on the outside, Raúl thinks.

In any case she was beautiful to him, whatever Raquel says. A fierce, inquisitive gaze, intense black eyes, and a slightly defiant attitude—when she wasn't talking like a ten-year-old girl that is. And Raúl wasn't making it up, since four other men had seen her beauty before him. Two of them dead now. Raúl, luckily, had ended up with the Julia of the aging, papery skin and sagging rear. If he'd got hold of her in the full loveliness of her youth, he thinks, he would have destroyed it.

Julia

This place is like a hammock. Very peaceful. Lovely. Water is transformation, water is everything. We are water. I wrote a book—prophetic, as it turned out—called *Water to Water*. The very mountains are a sea. I was able to understand myself in relation to everything else. I, arrogant like. . . Indomitable like water. Persistent like water too; audacious, perceptive, and also compassionate. Just like in that poem I wrote about fish suffocating in light. A lot of people thought it was the best thing I'd ever written. That's because I knew what the fish were feeling, thanks to my asthma. I don't agree though. In my view, everything of mine is of the same quality. It's like figuring a person has put less heart into some things than others. No. It all represents the same elevation, the same quest for excellence—I never cut corners. Raul was totally wrong about me. He couldn't love me and not love my poetry, and

I couldn't love him if he didn't. Nor could I stay with him out of compassion. If my leaving crushed him, that wasn't my problem. I wrote a poem in which I called him one-eyed because he'd only been able to see half of me. I am a whole, not a half. It's time for men to stop negating us and suffocating us and dumping us into the water. I've always been entire. And I fought tooth and nail not to suffocate, to remain whole. I fought just as violently as he sought to snuff me out.

It's a good thing I no longer remember anything, or it would make me really sad. All I ever wanted was to be myself. So then why...? Even women are sexist. Men enslave them on the inside, turning them into easy targets incapable of fighting for themselves. Diana, my own daughter, never forgave me, as if I were to blame for how I was built, as if I was supposed to evaporate or shrink or deny my talents so she didn't feel so much in my shadow. She couldn't understand that she had her own talents and could have shone with her own light, even if maybe it wasn't as bright as mine, and that's why she acted the way she did. A family always has room for more than one sun.

What time is it, there where time still exists?

There are things that would make you cry if you thought about them. I never cried for myself, never felt sorry for myself, despite

33

how distant I was from my mother as a girl. As a girl, and always, there was this distance between us. I endured it out of pride, and swallowed my tears. She was so beautiful and loving when she wanted to be, which was almost never. That taught me to be tough when necessary. And seeing her later, as an old woman, all grimy and ugly and hunched, bothered me a bit. If she hadn't caused me so much suffering as a little girl, so much that even my father had to intervene, I would have felt sorry for her. That's why, when thieves broke into her house in La Calera and beat her up for refusing to tell them where she kept her debit cards, I was happy despite myself and figured the thieves hadn't just been after the cards but had thought, like me, that she deserved a good thrashing. The servants had been involved, and before breaking in they'd poisoned the three dogs. The two maids, the driver, and the gardener all ended up in prison. They were photographed handcuffed together, covering their faces with their hands. Even so I felt a pang when I saw her in the hospital, wrinkled and sniveling, purple as a prune from the blows. On our way out my father and I commented on her appearance and felt sorry for her, yes, but also amused. He was the one who came up with the prune comparison. They'd been divorced a long time, but they saw each other occasionally.

My father is the person I loved most in life. We used to play golf and have lunch every Tuesday at the Los Lagartos club, which had a top-shelf chef. The best steak tartare I ever had. He was a real foodie, my father was. We were pals. Nobody appreciated my poetry and my voice the way he did. I would like to sing again, if I could. My father will continue to search for me, but he won't find me. He may be the person who misses me most on this earth.

Aleja

The homeless guy scattered all of the trash in front of the yoga academy, looked over at her, and started undoing his pants. He flashed her. He knew she was there behind the curtain. Breathe deep. Inhale. Exhale. Ahhhhhh. Inhale. Exhale. Ahhhhhh. Buddhism teaches us to feel neither disgust nor delight. Pig. Inhale. Ahhhhhh. The cops are useless in this country.

On Julia's ranch there's a Buddhist meditation center run by a very skinny, very tall man: the teacher. Aleja thinks he looks like Nosferatu, the vampire, though he's taller than Nosferatu. The day Aleja met him they talked about advanced breathing techniques and it was clear he knew a lot about the subject. He's a kind, powerful person. He teaches Zen meditation, but he knows yoga and plenty of other things. When Aleja visited the center the last time she was at Julia's, she talked with the people who live there, the monks, who told her that in the beginning, when they'd first opened, the locals used to say they were performing black masses and collecting children's blood to drink. Eventually they accepted the monks and even came to respect them. People like to hear themselves talk, Aleja thinks, and a lot of the time even when they don't believe what they're saying, they say it anyway.

She stayed at Julia's place several times—gorgeous spot. Because of the damp, it wasn't the healthiest climate for Julia, with her asthma. Raúl renovated the house for her—did a lovely job—and built a wooden deck with a beautiful bamboo railing that offered a view of the mountain chains, one behind the other, like a sea, Julia used to say. Well, curtains, more like; Aleja doesn't know where Julia came up with the damn sea comparison. She and Julia often talked about opening a branch of the yoga academy in the area. Daydreaming, that's all. Asanas on that deck were magical. The curtains of mountains spreading out before them and behind the house a high, steep crag covered with native vegetation. Humberto Fajardo, who is a rock climber and had ropes and carabiners and other gear, climbed it once and said he'd come across drawings of hands on a rock, traced who knows how many hundreds of years ago by the local indigenous people. He's a good-looking guy, Humberto is, with those athletic arms and legs

37

highlighted by his spandex clothing. He looked like a movie star in the Mini Morris he later traded for the Audi. He was always complimenting Aleja's body, and she taught him yoga and meditation. The two of them always had chemistry; honestly, a lot more than he and Julia did. Life sure is funny. He had tasteful tattoos on his arms, abstract designs that he got in New York, at the studio of an artist who's been featured in magazines, *Harper's*, that sort of thing. He buys beautiful shirts that he gets shipped from Italy, and when he rolls up his sleeves a bit the tattoos peek out. His films are beautiful—they're commercials, actually, but very artistic. Artistic advertising is the hardest kind, Aleja thinks, and the highest paid. He didn't need Julia's money, which is why he was able to claim it was all a lie ginned up to discredit him and sell tabloids and gossip magazines. They needed a scapegoat, and he refused to give them the pleasure—he's no idiot.

And he's come off well in the media, in the end.

After the first split, Julia worked for a long time as the chief creative officer of an ad agency, making a fortune. She was amazing at that job. As if she needed a fortune, with all her family money! Even so, she spent very little. Stingy, really, ever since high school. She'd met Humberto at the agency, but the romance didn't start till after her divorce from Raúl. She later told Aleja how foul-tempered and violent Humberto was and Aleja didn't believe it—after all, Julia said everybody was foul-tempered. Even Diego. Who knows if her claims about his foul temper were true. Most likely, Aleja thinks, it was that nobody could stand her. He's still doing photography, Aleja figures, because as far as she knows, he's still alive.

Raúl

From the airport they set out for Julia's ranch along a road that descended in tight switchbacks through mountains covered first with pines and eucalyptus, then giant ferns, Andean oaks, and trumpet trees, and then, as they arrived almost two hours later, dense bamboo groves and coffee fields shaded by pacay and Colombian walnut.

The property was ten acres with a large house designed by an architect with impeccable taste and very little personality. It sat at the foot of one of the bluffs that are so common in the area, where the fog is constantly blotting out and then retracing the outlines of the lush vegetation, native to such humid temperate climates, that covers them. These crags are part of the spurs that rise from the Bogotá plateau, like cliffs looming above an absent sea. Supposedly during battles the Spanish conquistadors forced indigenous warriors to retreat and drove them off the cliffs. That, Raúl realizes, would mean they'd fallen with their bows and arrows some two hundred meters right onto Julia's porch, or onto the patio, breaking their necks or smashing their skulls among the irises. The place doesn't have bad energy, just intense, willful energy, while Raúl's house is serene even though it's walled in by his bamboo and reeds, and by dense, ancient shade trees in the coffee fields that he stopped tending so they've turned jungly.

Iris Flower was the name of the book of poems that precipitated the collapse.

The cliff on Julia's property rises straight up, its base just twenty meters from the house. There's something gloomy about the place, Raúl thinks, and the lake in front of the porch, to the left of the deck, makes the darkness even deeper. Laguna Verde, it's called, and the trail is named after it. The green is from the tiny algae, very intensely colored, almost phosphorescent, that sometimes covers it. It's said to be more than fifty meters deep, but the truth is nobody has managed to measure the bottom. Reeds fill the banks and crowd the shallows, and the rest of it tends to get covered in algae that has to be cleared out every so often to keep it from smothering everything. Supposedly up until a few years ago you could catch blue-tinged fish with bulging eyes and spiny fins, but they were overfished or died out. The lake has a surface area of some three square kilometers, and Julia's property shares it with two other neighbors. Sometimes it is wreathed in mist so only the chimeric outline of the reeds is visible. The tilapia glow bright red against the water, which is so deep it's almost black. There was a boat pulled up on a little beach, but Raúl was hesitant to climb in because he's a big guy and might have tipped it over if he'd tried to take it rowing. He never saw anybody use it. Humberto Fajardo probably did later, since he's into that sort of thing.

The cliff is covered with giant ferns and trees that grow almost horizontal. Raúl has it in his head that the lake is as deep as the cliff is high. A great place for a poet, a faithful reflection of her spirit, Julia must have thought when she was buying it, but the truth is not everybody appreciates its magic. Since she wasn't around, shady Humberto sold it—cheap, apparently—to a former agronomy professor at the Universidad Nacional, retired, who, not long after buying it and moving in, ran over a five-year-old boy with his SUV as he was headed back. The place sure has a menacing edge to it! Unable to cope with the death, the man couldn't bear to keep living in the area; with his dreams turned to dust, he and his wife, who had been so enthusiastic when they arrived, left. Now the place sits empty, with a for-sale sign on the front door. The door is carved with birds; Raúl designed it and then had it made by a craftsman in Nobsa, Boyacá, who's a god with a chisel and a piece of wood. Every once in a while, Raúl thinks he should go take photos before something happens to it, but he never does. And the lake is alone for now, with Indian skeletons resting in peace on the muddy bottom or whatever it is that's down there. It would be nice if a Spanish conquistador or two were resting down there as well, Raúl thinks, in full armor and with a slender arrow in the chink of his eye or ear.

Raquel

Though she's been watching it fall for many years now, snow still seems almost miraculous to Raquel. *Snow Country*, that was the name of that novel, a real masterpiece, by Mishima—shame to have to read translations. Kawabata, not Mishima. All is quiet in Inwood and throughout Manhattan. It's four in the afternoon, and it could be six in the morning. There are no streets, only snow and children with dogs, all of them elated. There are no buses, no noise. Only Julián's farts, up in the apartment, which occasionally ring out as he reads in the hammock—to infuse the tableau with a bit of joy, as he says.

"Your *Ode to Joy*," Raquel says.

Julián is from the Caribbean, though his father was Spanish. Mixed-race mother. They dance to "Penas de amor." When Bienvenido is singing, "Ódiame" is life itself, but when it's Ecuadorians or Chileans it's suicide, Raquel thinks. "Hate me boundlessly, mercilessly," Bienvenido sings as some guy's erection sweeps across the dance floor, pressed firm against his partner. García Márquez wasn't able to convince anyone that his novel contained the tragedy of humankind. Nor does anybody believe Bienvenido to be so vast or merciless. In both cases you're left with a feeling of immortality and joy.

At Raquel's house, Raúl's the only one who doesn't know how to dance. Raquel's always thought it was funny that out of the five siblings, he's also the only one who looks like his mother. She was from Quibdó, part Indian, part Black, part white; she looked like she could have been South Asian. The others took after their father. Beautiful couple—the white man from Medellín, good-looking, son and grandson of racists, and the beautiful woman from Chocó, a high school teacher. A long and happy marriage. Julián and Raquel are parallel. In the United States the two of them are Black, and proud to be, even if they don't look it. The one-drop rule. One drop of Black blood and you're Black. The joke about the Puerto Rican who goes to Alabama, and a white man, for some reason, insults him and calls him a nigger. "I'm not a nigger! I'm Puerto Rican," the Boricua protests. "I don't care what kind of nigger you are," the white man replies. Politically correct people don't like that

45

joke—they think it's racist. Morons. A soda cracker could dance better than Raúl, but he does enjoy music. Julia was a really good singer, and he fell in love with that. In love up to the hilt, as they say. Handel arias, she sang, and Cuban nueva trova, which Julián likes and Raquel can't stand. Any idiot can sing, Raquel used to tell Raúl, even before Julia left him. Julia liked singing that song against the Chilean dictatorship, and Raquel would whisper to Raúl, "Look at her. Do you think she gives two figs what happened in Chile?"

Raquel claims not to like nueva trova, but whenever she hears Silvio Rodríguez she gets goosebumps. Just like with Woody Allen: she swears she's not going to laugh at his nonsense, but she can't resist.

Raúl

They arrived from the airport at about eleven in the morning, in a torrential downpour, and before Raúl managed to get his bearings, having gotten only the briefest glance of the ominous, jungly, waterlogged cliff, they were already inside each other, the two of them in a very dark room, not even bothering to open the windows with their louvered wooden shutters that blocked out the world's ten thousand phenomena. The woodwork in the house, like everything else about it, was high quality but without any particular charm. Outside were the tilapias, which Raúl hadn't seen yet—they would be swimming under the screen of near-phosphorescent algae in the dark, limpid water. It was like a bender, a delirium. When, at about noon, they managed at last to pull themselves apart and think about something besides their overwhelming love, and they opened the shutters, the mountains were blotted out by water, since rain was pelting down as far as the eye could see.

There wasn't a deck yet—Raúl would build that later—and they sat on Julia's porch to gaze out at everything, as it would become his habit to do months later on his own porch once he bought his own property and built the house. The ranch manager's wife brought him coffee. Julia was singing somewhere, and Raúl felt happy. Returning to his homeland brought him peace—the beauty of the place, the ever-shifting shades of gray of the cloudbursts in the distant mountains, the green of the immediate surroundings, and the immense luck of having her.

They stayed to live on the ranch and Julia traveled to Bogotá only occasionally to deal with career-related matters. Raúl basically abandoned his place in Cucunubá and started working from Julia's instead. He built beautiful things during that period, just so she would admire them. A little suspension footbridge over the Lapas, still used by the locals, to which Julia didn't contribute a peso. He paid for all of it, apart from a small sum from the local government. He used cables made of braided reed fiber and columns composed of stalks of bamboo lashed together with the same kind of cable, which could have withstood the weight of the entire National Army, an army that, as it happened, was starting to have a major presence in the region at the time, since guerrilla fighters were supposedly attempting to establish a front in the area, parts of which are densely wooded and wild.

Julia kept a fancy anthology of Rubén Darío poems on the toilet tank and hung photos of herself in the library. Red flags of that sort piled up, ominously fluttering signals that there was some deep error or misunderstanding in the very fact that they were a couple, and Raúl didn't see them, blind as a mole, besotted as an ape. The princess is sad, full stop. End of poem. Whether to put down the book or keep reading as the fetid stench intensifies? It's tragic, if you think about it: he loved her, but the books on the toilet and the way she went about promoting her so-called career meant that, without realizing it, he gradually lost respect for her and started seeing her as the ten-year-old girl she sometimes became. His love for her didn't go away, though—that only increased.

The bathroom had a stained-glass window with a lily pattern, intricate, skillful, beautifully done.

How did it get to be four in the afternoon?! When everything fills up with fog, like right now, Raúl, already sitting quietly in the chair on his porch, gets even quieter and the world seems to shake free of the laws of time. Bamboo blotted out by the fog. Heart wounds, deep ones, nearly healed and erased over time. Not even scars are eternal. Once Raúl broke a crown and he told the dentist he'd always thought that crowns lasted forever.

"Nothing lasts forever," the dentist had replied.

Imagine learning such a truth in the dentist's chair! Dentists know it all too well because they see it every day, Raúl thought. Teeth are the most transitory things there are.

He has pending tasks piled up on his drawing board—there's never a shortage of them—but if he didn't take these long stretches on the porch, his work would flow less easily. Recently he has been designing some rural bus stops, which will never be completed, or maybe they will, you never know. Wrought iron and bamboo. Raúl goes to the Zen Buddhism center from time to time, and what they do there is exactly the same as him sitting on the porch. He goes because he likes the people and sometimes needs a bit of social interaction, but he prefers his leather chair, finds all the incense, bowing, and song-and-dance superfluous.

Aleja always said the head teacher at the center looked like Nosferatu. And actually, if you really looked at him, he did. Julia was missing, and Aleja and her beautiful body never came around anymore. One day, Raúl saw the teacher walking toward the meditation hall dressed in his black robes, and since it was foggy and the teacher is extremely tall and thin, he seemed to float like the legendary count. A lot of people don't like him because he tends to be blunt. Cruel, some say. A self-appointed Zen master, a fraud, they say. Raúl doesn't care. They talk about countryside things, he and the teacher do, and Raúl has realized the old man knows a lot about plants and trees. As far as he can tell, he is wise and kindly. Just like Dracula. He commissioned Raúl to build a long book-case made of cedar and bamboo—the teacher sketched the design himself, noting down the measurements and the kind of varnish— to create storage for those round cushions they sit on to meditate. Raúl decorated it with some copper inlays, which did not clash with the wood but instead looked like they'd been there forever.

Julia

No one can tell me I didn't love him. Of course I loved him. Why should my love have to last forever? While I was in love, I wrote a book for him by hand, thirty poems, which was later issued by a publisher specializing in high-quality, handbound volumes of poetry, real works of art. The book got some attention in the newspapers. Short articles, of course—it was poetry, after all—way back in the arts section, but it made me happy all the same.

I should have seen what was happening with Raúl way back then. I would give him the poems, he'd read them aloud. They were love poems, and I didn't realize that his already irritating façade of kindness was masking total indifference—I mean, total, total indifference. Raúl used to tell me he loved me, but it took me some time to realize that he didn't like my art, because the woman he had fallen in love with was not me. We can be so blind sometimes! He was in love with another woman—the woman he loved wasn't me. If he didn't love my poetry, that meant he didn't love me either— even though people told me later that Raúl almost died when I left him. "You murdered the poor guy," Aleja told me—she has a tendency to stick her nose in other people's business. "I don't give a shit what you think," I retorted. "There are things a person has to do to maintain their self-respect."

Hemingway used to say that you write better when you're in love. Of course, I wasn't a big fan of Hemingway because he was such a chauvinist. I wrote the poems for Raúl out on the ranch after coming back from New York, and I started the book of water. In *El Espectador* I was referred to as one of the country's premier poets. The critic—a man—exhibited a certain reluctance, seeming to want to contain or disguise his enthusiasm, but I was happy about it anyway, since I didn't want to get pigeonholed as an erotic writer. Even though there were moments of intense eroticism in the Raúl poems, the deep contemplation of things was foremost, and that's not what critics expect from female poets. I refused to stick to eroticism. Women always cooking or making love. Ridiculous. From the kitchen to the bedroom and back again. Not me. I rebelled, I paid the price, and now I can't look at fish because, as García Lorca said, *I am no longer myself, and my house is no longer my house.*

Not even my face is my face anymore.

If I were myself, I would know what time it is there where time still exists. I would sing.

Aleja

When they used to come over to Aleja's for a visit, Raúl would sit on the sofa and Julia would sit on his lap. As a yogi, Aleja believes that physical well-being endows us with eternal youth, but it was still pretty weird seeing a portly fifty-year-old man with a forty-something woman perched on his lap. Plus, he was shy—not really the sort to carry his girlfriend around. But he was in love and he looked happy.

Now that the pig has gone away for a minute, the girl should take the opportunity to go out and pick up the crap he left strewn around. There we go. She's out there—didn't even have to tell her. She's a good girl, seems like, but you never know around here. She hasn't been on the job long. Julia's mother's employees had been with her for more than fifteen years and ended up in prison. The robbers beat her up good, and nobody can figure out why they gave her such a thrashing, let alone how she managed not to die or break anything. Once the swelling and bruising faded, she looked exactly the same—in other words, all made up. Julia used to say that every time she saw her mother, she had an asthma attack from all the face powder. More a psychosomatic response, Aleja thinks. Whenever Raúl spent time with Julia's mother, at lunches or other such affairs, it was obvious why the couple wasn't going to make it. They had absolutely nothing in common. The old woman was like an extraterrestrial to Raúl, and vice versa, and Julia was more like her than she imagined, poor thing. You could tell how hard he had to work trying to fit into that whole scene with her parents and family. Aleja doesn't think Raúl ever wanted to go to the club. All he thinks about is his bamboo and his adobe and his wattle and daub.

Raúl

Whenever they were in Bogotá, Julia and Raúl used to take the opportunity to go to movies, concerts, or exhibitions. Or she would take the opportunity, really, because Raúl found the movies, poetry readings, and other events to be more a bother than anything else. But he went along for her.

And so he'd sit there in his seat, slowly going mad, like he was locked up in a tiny, stuffy room. He didn't give a damn about the plots, and he thought actors were fakers, bad liars. Complete crap. Even Robert De Niro struck him as a fraud, and he'd say as much to Julia, who would get annoyed, of course. She couldn't have had a worse companion for going to the movies. When it came to the seventh art and all the other arts, it was a miracle she didn't leave him earlier. Fortunately for him, she didn't tell him he was out of luck if he didn't like Robert De Niro.

When they went to Berlin, their first trip together after coming back from New York, she planned out their itinerary every day and had a list of things they had to do before they returned to Bogotá. Raúl was like a docile gorilla trailing a vivacious little monkey, standing in line for an hour and a half outside the parliament building. Gorilla and monkey visiting the Schiele exhibition, which ended up knocking his socks off. But it all blew up in a huge fight right at the end of the trip, the day after her reading. *Vegetal Steel*, it was called. It was no Woodstock, but it wasn't to an empty room either, since vegetal steel has its admirers everywhere. At the end of the ten days, Raúl, oversaturated with all the guided tourism, lost his temper and flew off the handle, yelling at her—he doesn't remember why, anything could have set him off by then—at a photography exhibition, with people staring at them. *Topography of Horror*, the show was called. The pudgy Latin American with large, gleaming eyes, demented, and the furious little monkey—never one to run away from a fight—berated each other in front of a photo of Hitler saluting his troops. Raúl hadn't wanted to see photos of those psychopaths. He didn't want to hear about Goering or Goebbels or any of that, whereas for her it was an obligatory stop, maybe so she could write a poem later. He could have throttled her.

His famous rages.

Sonia, with her spectacular green eyes, is twenty-one years his junior, and so far they haven't had a single big blowup. He does get a little annoyed with the way she's always asking him questions, as if he knew lots of things he doesn't know, but that's as far as it's gone. Sonia spends her time reading the books in the library and making the house look nice, while he sits on the porch or at his work table, busy with his own thing. And the property is jam-packed with flowers: irises on the patio, since Sonia loves them as much as Julia did; balsam everywhere—*Impatiens walleriana* it's called, and Raúl has no idea where the impatiens bit came from, since the plants are no trouble at all to grow; must be they're impatient to bloom—lilies, white ones and brightly colored ones too; hydrangeas, roses, azaleas . . . "This place is so dark," Sonia said when she first arrived, and she started planting things along the paths through the bamboo, on the patio, everywhere. Impatiens and irises can thrive in dim light, their flowers brightening the shadows from within.

Sonia wasn't the least bit bothered that Julia had loved irises too. She didn't give a damn about Julia's existence or nonexistence. The first book from the library that she read was *Crime and Punishment*. And when Raúl saw how much she'd enjoyed it, he recommended she read Cain, Chandler, and so on—noir is his favorite—and Sonia read them, but she didn't see the appeal. Why, for example, do the detectives and everybody else in those novels drink so much? Marlowe got on her nerves. She said he probably reeked of booze and body odor. Sonia doesn't get black humor; she's the sort of person who's always doing what she can to appear on the side of light—just like her damn impatiens, whose gaudy colors Raúl sometimes finds dizzying. And she doesn't curse, no filthy language. Raquel's vocabulary would give her a jolt. Sonia read all of Dostoevsky and then kept going with the other Russians—Tolstoy, Turgenev, Gogol. The complete works of Aguilar, on rice paper with a leather binding, which you have to clean regularly because they turn green from the damp air. Raúl never imagined a flight attendant could be such a bookworm. Right now she's on *Death in Venice* and has *Buddenbrooks* and the rest of them queued up. She's like a sugar mill chewing up cane. His dad could have left them money instead of books, and they'd be loaded. And Sonia uses the back of the toilet not for Rubén Darío tomes, thank God, but for floral arrangements with a Japanese flair, assembled using a little ring of spikes under a sort of bamboo lattice that he designed according to her instructions and had made in Bogotá. When he met her, Raúl was still taking psych meds and sleeping pills because he hadn't yet emerged from his brutal depression over everything that had gone down with Julia. He met her on a TACA plane—the accident-prone airline—flying back from Leticia. She was twenty-eight; she's twenty-nine now. Raúl showed her photos of the property, which he had on his laptop, and Sonia said she'd like to live in a place like that. She'd been raised in the countryside, she said, and she was getting bored with her job. They ran into some turbulence and she sat down next to him until the plane stopped lurching and steadied again. "Come whenever you like," Raúl told her. "You don't even have to sleep with me if you don't want." She quit her job and now they're out on his ranch.

Raquel

When Raúl told Raquel that his relationship with Julia had been a
horrible two-and-a-half-year misunderstanding, Raquel responded:
Misunderstanding my ass, first Julia seduced you and then she got
bored and wanted to be rid of you. You men are so naïve. Women
can destroy you with a snap of their fingers.

Raquel visited Julia's blog a few times and found some poems
that bragged about having murdered him. In them, Julia talked
about killing the things they'd loved together: the Nevado del
Tolima volcano, which is visible, rising perfect as Mount Fuji,
from the balcony at Raúl's place, the ninny murdered that; and
the bamboo on the property, "which is like a sea," she murdered
that too. And she ends by saying, "him as well, murdered," with
the tremendous arrogance of someone who is certain of having
inflicted mortal harm on another person. And now look—how

ironic. Because Raquel doesn't believe Julia's going to be found at all, much less found alive.

Raquel keeps the Raúl murder poems in a trunk—Julia wrote a bunch of them, and she printed them out. Rummaging for them, she instead comes across the photo of her mother beaming in front of the hydrangeas in the front garden of the house in Teusaquillo. No wonder there was an empty spot in the album. Raquel herself must have pulled out the photo from there, who knows when or why. Once she's started looking through the trunk, she could keep going forever. She is struck by the gloominess of the holy cards with images of the saints and text in Italian fixed to the inside of the lid. The trunk had belonged to immigrants; she and Julián bought it in an antique shop in the Bronx, and the original owners are now not just dead but forgotten. Raquel uses it to store photos, Verizon statements, random coins, subway tokens, ancient subway maps, silver dollars, letters she never sent (from back when people still wrote letters), computer cables, newspaper clippings. What a beautiful smile her mother had! So like Raúl's. The snow is falling hard now. The brooch Julián gave her, here it is, pure Caribbean style, like a cockroach made of precious stones. Raquel looked so elegant with her cockroach brooch the one night she wore it. "The next time you feel like buying me jewelry, I'll come with," she told

Julián. And her mother, you see, a beautiful Black woman, had amazing taste. Intelligent, well-educated, sophisticated. If Raquel were a drinker, she would have a whiskey right now as a way of savoring the blizzard . . . On the 12th, her mom will have been dead for six years. Last year, two days before the anniversary of her death, a vase she had given them fell in the living room without anyone touching it. Fear and joy. It did not break. It is a sign. Raquel actually envies people who drink, but she thinks whiskey tastes vile. She would have a tiny drink in honor of her mother, here in the middle of the snowstorm. Aguardiente, with its licorice flavor, is even worse. Thinking about her still makes Raquel want to cry.

Here they are.

"Him, murdered"—yes, that's what she wrote.

Evil, stupid, and half-mad, Raquel thinks. Hopefully she's had an awful time of it, wherever she is.

"No! I didn't say that," she mutters, alarmed. "I didn't say anything."

Julia

This place is like a hammock, stable and fluid—how lovely. Shame about feeling like bursting into tears. I was never much for weeping and I'm not about to start now. I sometimes used to cry over animals, it's true—such helplessness, my God, and such human cruelty. The emaciated horse struggling to pull a cart along a street in Bogotá or a dog I once saw on the side of the road, standing next to another dog that had just been killed by a car. Raúl didn't seem to really get why I couldn't stop crying, not even after I told him what I'd seen. And when I left Raúl I cried for two days straight. That was my mourning. My way of making peace with myself. My nostalgia for all the lovely moments we had together.

That first year was particularly beautiful. It was as if the two of us were creating everything around us, building it from scratch. I published two books that year, both well received, and started writing two others. We lived more at his place than mine, or on my ranch, I don't know why. I think he wasn't a big fan of the powerful energy that the places I live in possess. Or maybe my place and I, together, intimidated him. Divide and you will conquer, I'd say, kidding, of course, because I liked his place as much as I did mine and felt just as at home there.

All of the men I've been with ended up being afraid of me, and I ended up getting a little bored with them. Nobody rules her own heart. Well, not all of them; Juan Mario left me, and the pain of that abandonment was vast. A great painter, not as renowned as he deserved, but renowned in the art world, at any rate. All of my husbands were artists. Later on Juan Mario got sick—schizophrenia. At least he didn't die like the other two. The last time I saw him he was doing pretty well, somewhat coherent, though he looked haggard. His teeth were wrecked from the medication. He didn't feel like talking much and didn't even congratulate me for my recent successes. The girls' father wasn't an artist. The only one. Attorney for an oil company. Leukemia. I went to visit him in the hospital and he looked dead already, suffocated, with his eyes wide and staring—I don't think he even recognized me, already on his death bed, poor man. His second wife looked at me askance, but she looks askance at anybody who seems unconventional in any way, at all out of the ordinary. She's one of those docile women who worship their husbands. Not at all right for him.

And it's possible that Juan Mario got sick because of me. My power affects men in unexpected ways.

Aleja

Katerina donned a mask and latex gloves to pick up the trash
that animal had scattered around. When Aleja was a little girl,
the servant girls had chapped hands, braids, long skirts, and gold
earrings, and they came from Boyacá—it was as if it were still the
colonial era. And look how pretentious this one is now, bragging
about being a nurse and talking all fancy. She earns as much as a
nurse in any case. If you add up not just her base salary but also all
the perks and whatnot, she's collecting a politician's salary. Human
greed. As a yogi, you're supposed to let go of material attachments.
It's a process of relinquishment, of giving, of opening up and not
clinging, but the more people have, the more they cling to it. Diana
was better at that than Julia. The girl's not poor, far from it, since
not everything of Julia's will go to Humberto—who's her legiti-
mate spouse at the moment, regardless of what people say—and

her two girls will get half. But the gossip rags stuck their noses in and made a mess of everything. They even painted Diana to be a suspect. She'll end up wealthy eventually, but she's charging Aleja a bundle to run the Santa Bárbara location all the same. And since there aren't a lot of qualified instructors running around, she gets away with it. Greed drives us to material, emotional, mental, and physical attachment. It causes us to identify with things, preventing us from seeing the reality of who we truly are.

That filthy pig is back! Look at him! And the girl hasn't even noticed. Come inside, come inside. She's not going to hear me unless I smash the window. Now she's talking to him! Smiling and everything. Next thing you know she'll be bringing him coffee and pastries. Idiot. Come inside, come inside! She's pretending not to hear me . . . No!

He's helping her clean it all up!

Raúl

They returned from the Berlin trip in silence, stunned by what had happened at that nightmarish exhibition. A sad end to the honeymoon. Luckily, starting the renovations at Julia's house distracted her and helped them slowly reconcile and begin to take pleasure in each other again.

Since no one else was available, Raúl hired Braulio to do the work, which he later came to regret. The dovetailed pine ceiling, ugly and clumsily installed, was replaced with a cane ceiling with a semi-matte varnish. The bathroom off the master bedroom was expanded and got a tub and a small papyrus garden. Three months of joy and peace. Love restored. They built the deck so they could go out front and contemplate the mountain ranges that stretched out one behind the other, like layers of stage curtains, to the Magdalena River Valley, and thus escape from the troubled energy that the cliff cast over the house, an oppressive feeling that persisted there—these things don't go away—but which was much less noticeable on the luminous expanse of the front deck.

Sonia goes by just then, sweeping the leaves the wind has deposited on the porch's tiled floor, and Raúl admires her dress, which is long and fitted, magenta blue, and sleeveless. With her thick, curly black hair and her tawny shoulders, she looks like a young Roman noblewoman.

Raúl spends a lot of time in his chair on the porch, especially on rainy days like this. During big downpours, he drops what he's doing in the workshop or at his drawing table and goes out to be with them, to watch them fluctuate, and also to listen to the Lapas, which tumbles torrentially among the rocks not far away, roaring with its many resonances.

A little while back he finalized the design for a sugar jar made of polished coconut shell, which Sonia loved. The base is going to be a curved piece of bamboo, as is the handle on the lid. Spoon made of macana palm, and a little twig of bamboo as a handle. The coconut ends up burnished and dappled, vaguely resembling tortoiseshell. Raúl had already designed the coordinating saltcellar and had it made; it consisted of half a Colombian walnut shell topped by a lid made from the other half, plus a little spoon made of half a corozo nut with holes drilled in it for sprinkling the salt. Its handle was bamboo too. Very pretty. But a disaster. Because it's so humid, the salt clumps up and doesn't flow. And Raúl can't produce a saltcellar that works only in arid regions. He'll figure something out. Maybe the artisans who made the prototypes will come up with something. The "pilot saltcellar," as the pedants from the NGOs would say, using that graceless language they're so fond of. The artisans live in La Esperanza, next to the abandoned train station, and they do good work, but they're unreliable and you have to be patient with them.

Sonia also liked the prefabricated houses for poor families that Raúl designed about two months ago. He decorated the seams of the concrete panels with Guadua bamboo, and some panels are made just of Guadua. They ignored his idea of using palm thatch roofs in the hotter regions. The project was financed by a Belgian organization seeking to assist needy families; it was rather bureaucratic and rigid. They dismissed the thatch idea out of hand; they wanted to use the same model of house in the hotter regions that they did in the uplands, because they're cheaper to produce that way. So the tenants in hot places could go fuck themselves. Unfortunately, Raúl thinks, those tenants love concrete too and would rather roast on the banks of the Cauca under a ferrocement roof than suffer the seeming humiliation of having a thatch one. It's some small comfort to know that as long as they're going to be roasting in his houses, at least the houses are pretty.

Spoons, bridges, schools, chapels. Better to have more than one thing going at once. Raquel calls Raúl the Leonardo da Vinci of vegetable matter. He'd dream up a bamboo helicopter. A war machine made of macana palm and reeds. Raúl's weak jokes, like this reed one, started grating on Julia's nerves. He grated on her nerves more and more, and she grated on Raúl's. They soon got to a point where he had to tread very carefully, tiptoeing around to avoid triggering a fight. He was terrified by the thought of losing her, knowing it might kill him, and he was cautious in everything he said or did, not wanting to set her off. But he always set her off anyway, inadvertently, and in his frustration he would erupt and come very close to slapping her in the face and finally bringing it all crashing down. What an ending, with that kind of suspended torment. Whenever things got to that point, Raúl would stay quiet to keep her from guessing what was going through his mind, and then she'd get upset about his silence.

Julia wasn't much for jokes, weak or otherwise, unless they were old standards or ones she'd come up with herself. Other people's humor annoyed her; it made her feel vulnerable.

Deep-thinking poets don't go around being entertained by dumb bullshit like the helicopter joke. Humorless people are a menace to society, Raúl thinks. He's happy now to know he will never see her again. The memory of her produces a visceral revulsion, like what some people feel toward particular foods that have made them ill in the past, but her image still haunts him. He knows that tomorrow's her birthday, for example. The date will always loom over him; it's a curse. He no longer carries on arguments with her in his head, at least, the way he did day and night for almost a year after she left him, or insult her or berate her.

His grief is over.

Wherever she is, she's better off, and he hopes she will continue to pull further away, falling deeper and deeper into oblivion.

Aleja

The girl didn't bring the beggar coffee and pastries, but she did give him some leftover food wrapped in aluminum foil and a little Coca-Cola bottle full of milk. He's going to keep rummaging in the garbage, but he won't scatter it around, Katerina says—probably won't expose himself again, Aleja hopes—and they're going to give him milk and leftovers every day. He might go along with it. Exhibitionism is an illness. Humberto is going to crack up at this story. And would you look at that, the girl turned out to be pretty smart. The homeless guy'll end up going vegetarian, since we don't eat dead things in this house. It's pelting down rain again—this is the Great Flood. There's been flooding all over the country; the Cauca and the Magdalena have overspilled their banks, and the hydrologists at IDEAM say it's going to last a while. Right when we're supposed to be enjoying summer in all its glory. Not everybody accepts vegetarians. They say they're tedious, causing problems wherever they go. Not Aleja. She even eats meat if there's no other option. "You're the first vegetarian I've ever met who eats pork," Humberto teased her. Diana, Julia's girl, is vegan. She doesn't eat cheese or wear leather—and she's not wrong, since there's no valid reason to make a calf suffer just so we can have shoes. But we shouldn't take everything to the extreme either, because then it becomes impossible to live in society with other people. She doesn't wear wool clothing out of respect for the sheep—now that's something.

Julia used to get irritated with Aleja's vegetarianism, to say nothing of Diana's veganism. Julia always said vegetarians had papery skin and were pale like vampires. When she got something in her head, there was no getting it out again. She didn't even notice that Aleja had the opposite problem: she gets as red as a farmhand and has to wear face powder. And Julia was one to talk, with her skin like parchment and cellulitis on her ass! When she woke up in the morning she looked like a witch, a harpy, like her mother without makeup. But men were still attracted to her because of her strong personality. Maybe too strong, Aleja would say. Diana is a pain with that stuff, refusing to eat soup if a bone has been boiled in it for flavor, refusing to sleep under wool blankets

. . . She doesn't look like a vampire either—she has a healthy glow. When she travels, which she loves to do, she sometimes ends up going hungry and becomes a real grouch. And with all the working out she does, she has to take a lot of supplements to build muscle mass. Bogotá is nice when the sun's out. When it's raining day and night, it gets you down. Sometimes it feels like day will never come or that everything is under water. Dawn and dusk indistinguishable. She was arrogant, Aleja thinks. Even the birds don't sing here. Poor Julia. The beggars must get so cold at night. Maybe the layer of dirt on them keeps them warm.

Raquel

It gets light out and then dark and the snow keeps falling. Last year they had a big snowstorm, not nearly as big as this one, and afterward the temperature went up to almost fifty and then dropped again. The partially melted snow turned to ice, very dangerous. Half of the elderly population in the five boroughs broke their hips, including Albor, Raquel's neighbor and friend, who isn't even old yet, though he's headed there fast.

Julián has poured himself a glass of whiskey on the rocks and fallen asleep in the hammock, with *Leaves of Grass* on his belly. Translated by Borges, and not such a good translation either, Raquel thinks. Once Julián starts drinking, he can't stop, and he goes down in flames within an hour, two max, like one of those fireworks stands that used to catch fire outside of Bogotá. As a boy, Raúl blew off two fingertips on his left hand with a bottle rocket.

They hadn't moved to Bogotá yet. Medellín ended up outlawing fireworks and sky lanterns after that. The sky lanterns looked so beautiful sailing above the mountains and mingling with the stars. During the Giuliani era the city banned the firecrackers traditionally used in Chinatown's dragon festival. A dragon with no firecrackers is a real bummer. Everything with any life to it ends up getting adjusted to meet stodgy gringo norms. In East River Park the Puerto Ricans had these gorgeous handmade roulettes painted in a primitivist style, just like the ones Raquel and Raúl saw as kids on Colombia's Atlantic coast. They, too, disappeared, never to be seen again, along with the Bacardi they used to sell in little paper cups. Illegal! Illegal! Illegal! Of course the Boricuas were always making a huge ruckus in the park, Eddie Santiago blasting people's eardrums, and the trash they left strewn around was even worse. Raquel remembers how excited Raúl got—this was back during his apprenticeship—when she took him to see them. That day (officially a spring day even though there were still clumps of dirty snow in the corners) she first met Julia, who hugged her as if they were the best of friends. It really rubbed Raquel the wrong way, even though she generally likes people on principle. Even when they screw her over and show their true colors, she likes them. Everybody but Julia. A person without true colors would be like a dragon without firecrackers, Raquel thinks. Those lovely lines of poetry—how did they go? *With some I feel kinship because of their character qualities and with others I feel kinship because they lack those qualities.* One of her students is obsessed with Pessoa and thinks he's some sort of saint. *I feel kinship with superior men because they are superior, and I feel kinship with inferior men because they are superior too.* To each their own. Her mother became a saint. But there was something about Julia that Raquel didn't like—an appalling selfishness concealed behind the childish fawning she occasionally deployed to win people over. In love with herself and herself alone. She would have killed for the sake of her so-called career.

Raúl

After a few hours on the porch watching the rain fall, Raúl is convinced that nothing is solid. Everything is an illusion—a tremendous cliché, but not so easy to actually absorb, since mountains generally seem solid, and rocks, hard. There exists something that had no beginning and will have no end, even though it dwells within the mountains and the rocks and the water and the air and is as insubstantial as all of these. Eventually, that came to be his religion. Nothing of what we see has much reality to it, but some element that does resides in everything we see. "Our volcano," Julia used to call the Nevado del Tolima, visible in all its imposing perfection from the deck of her house and from the balcony at Raúl's, as long as it's not raining or overcast. And that's how he thought of it too, full of dreams as he was, but the volcano turned to smoke; she herself turned to nothing, turned to water, turned to mud, turned to fog. You have to sit stock-still to see it. You move the slightest bit, and things cling to that illusion of solidity.

That's the thing about bamboo. It does not seek solidity; on the contrary, it wants to be air. The nothingness of reeds waving in the breeze, Raúl thinks. Air within, air without. Thickset though Raúl may be, practically his entire body, if not all of it, is empty, like a stalk of bamboo. He is only noise. The booming void. The flatulent void. The nice thing about living alone is you're free to let them rip and shake the windowpanes. With Sonia around, he has to be careful and make sure she isn't nearby; given the age difference, there's no room for him to let his guard down. Luckily, she spends all her time out in the grove. One day she heard him and started laughing. "The three indispensable accessories of old codgers," Sonia said. "Farts, house slippers, and the daily paper." Raúl likes slippers, though he hasn't had any since he was a boy. There are some shaped like animals. He can just see himself sitting there with two huge bunnies on his feet—Flemish giants, given how big his feet are, and fuchsia-colored to cheer him up and bring some light to the darkness of the endless rain. And he hasn't read a newspaper in ages, or listened to the news. Reporters are always trying to make you believe a million things are happening, when in fact nothing at all is happening. There's this one radio station where the presenter announces the time every minute, in a tone of extreme urgency, and then comes some huge piece of news or the huge continuation of huge news. Time, news, time, news . . . That's the format. The listener ends up exasperated, enervated. History rockets away, impelled to unnatural speeds by those hooligans. As Raúl sees it, the last news worth mentioning was the end of the Second World War. Or the death of Christ, if you want to get picky about it. "Five p.m.: News alert! Jesus of Nazareth has died. Soldiers who had been guarding him stated that the alleged savior died after uttering a few incoherent words . . . Five-oh-one p.m.: Breaking! Pilate denies responsibility for the unfortunate events. In a press release, the civil servant claimed . . . Five-oh-two: The two thieves who accompanied him in his suffering . . ."

Julia

I have to stay so still! I had my faults, like anyone, I accept that, but I didn't do anything to deserve this. It is peaceful, though—I'd be lying if I said otherwise. At least I can console myself that I knew love and I knew triumph, and even though I ended up drowned, they had to work hard for it, manhandling me and avoiding my gnashing teeth—I was never a coward. I never liked weaklings, and though I sometimes melted, like I was a little girl again, it was always out of tenderness or compassion. Out of my own humanity. Like with those animals, poor things. The skinny horses pulling carts in Bogotá. Poor widdle fings! I had to get out and hug them. So saaaad! They destroyed me. I had to snap Manuela out of it, my own daughter, to make her cast off the feminine fragility that used to drive me nuts sometimes. The girl was born that way— nothing to be done about it. When she was six, Manuela hated the sand at the beach. She would run away shrieking from crickets and even butterflies. Ha, ha, ha. And while Diana was leaping around dressed any old way, Manuela was always neat as a pin—she couldn't stand feeling disheveled. It's in a person's DNA. Her paternal grandmother was exactly the same. Diana did start taking more care with her appearance, and dressing well—she had good taste, after all—but only as a teenager. I don't resent her even if she resents me. Anyone who saw us together would have thought we loved each other, and maybe we did, but it was a complicated love, full of anger and jealousy. Like a plant covered in those little lice they get. My love for Manuela was very intense, and maybe Diana was bitter about that, even though she loved her as much I did. I thought she was beautiful, Manuela was, and my eyes would glow when I looked at her, even after she was all grown. I wrote a poem. So delicate and moving! Why was everything so prickly and full of thorns? Why is my voice today the voice of nobody, the voice of water? My poor father has been running all over the place because people claim to have seen me in one city or another, and since he refuses to give up on finding me, he keeps traveling, searching for me and paying private eyes and informants full of malice or greed. Why has everything suddenly lost its color?

From: Raquel
Date: Tuesday, January 10, 6:32 p.m.
To: Adela
Subject: Assorted bullshit
Attachment: Photo

Impressive! The same thing just happened to me! That photo of my mom turned up in a trunk where it had no business being. It's a little scary, even if it has to do with her, right? Raúl says the two of us like to pretend we're witches and imagine things, but I think it happens to other people too and they simply don't notice.

As for the other thing you were asking about . . . The girl-friend's a stewardess, or was. Flight attendant. Very pretty, yes, much prettier than that poet who's nowhere to be found. I'm attaching the girl's photo, which I got from Raúl.

The poet was arrogant, an awful poet, and she practically killed him. It was just Raúl's luck—bad luck, as it turned out—to fall in love with a wannabe poet, social climber, and underachiever par excellence. He thought she was beautiful, but she wasn't, not in the way people mean when they say beautiful. A common wild-flower rather than a rose. But anyway, given what happened, that doesn't matter now—it's the least of our worries.

I've got a feeling something really terrible happened. It's been almost a month, and nothing. There aren't any guerrillas in that area, Raúl said, since for a while there were rumors that her last husband—her sixth, apparently, if you can believe it—a dirtbag from a good family, the kind of playboy you see splashed across the tabloids, had sold her to the guerillas. The guerrillas are blamed for everything in this country, and people who are guilty of so many things deflect responsibility. The embezzlers would point their fingers at the guerrillas if they could.

Sold her, my ass! He's the one who did something to her, I say. The guerrillas would rather have gone after that daddy's boy instead. The police have been questioning him, anyway—how could they not? He's the husband. But you know what the police are like down there. There were some ransom demands, all fake, Raúl said. They also think it's possible she's hiding out somewhere, the way people with severe depression sometimes take off and start a new life really far away—Buenos Aires, Boca Raton, Manizales—with a new identity. Seriously, though. Somebody claimed to have seen a woman who looked a lot like her, only unkempt and filthy, who was sitting in a pew in the Manizales cathedral, singing beautifully. But Julia didn't strike me as depressed. I get the impression that . . . I don't even know how to describe it. You know what I mean. And what's rough is I'm hardly ever wrong about these things. Just now as I was staring at the cushion of snow piled up on the fire escape, something came over me. The snow gleams as if it were alive. Cold and alive, know what I mean? Scary. It's like we don't know anything about the world, don't have any idea what this place is that we inhabit—we're as defenseless as children. And suddenly there are things like the snow on the rusty fire escape or a gust of wind and rain against the windowpane, and you have to keep it together not to feel panic—or terror, really.

What was the other thing you were asking? Oh, right. Here's how to make mofongo: Take six plantains, still really green. They're probably not easy to find in Saskatoon, but at this point you can get them pretty much anywhere in the world . . .

Aleja

You shouldn't open just one additional academy, Aleja, Humberto told her, you should think about building out an entire chain. He'd be willing to invest, and now Aleja has to pump the brakes on him, because he's all hyped up and going to see locations downtown and up north in Suba, and recruiting additional investors from among his marketing buddies. Aleja tells him not to even dream about expanding that fast, since Diana's their only qualified yoga instructor—she despises him, by the way, just like Manuela does—and Humberto says that's never been a problem, they'll just train some more. They can find women to run the new locations among their own clientele. Aleja would rather take things slow, and she doesn't want to mix friendship and work, emotions and work, sex and work, but everything Humberto's saying is so sensible, so well considered. And it's also true that things have always worked out well for him, thanks to his business instinct, and that's why he's so wealthy today, despite what wagging tongues may say. Because envy is always in plentiful supply. Of course Aleja would prefer he didn't meddle so much, but she can't figure out how to tell him that, and the fact that his ideas are so fantastic makes it even more difficult. The thirty million pesos Aleja lent him are another matter. That's personal, nothing to do with his professional undertakings. It's always best to keep things separate—otherwise it's chaos and you can't figure out what the hell is going on. And Humberto himself was the one who insisted on paying that high interest rate. He's so lovely. So handsome. With that deep voice that caresses your ear. Yesterday he asked her to please lend him another ten million, since he was still a bit illiquid, just temporarily, and Aleja had to lie and say she didn't have it. He can't be short on cash, given he has all those CDs Julia left him. It's not that Aleja is worried about the thirty million—no, she knows he's good for it, it's chump change to him.

He's supposed to make his first interest payment next Tuesday.

Raúl

The six months it took to build Raúl's house were calm ones. Misunderstandings arose occasionally, but they were resolved relatively quickly; once the construction was completed, they became increasingly frequent, intense, and difficult to resolve. He'd get on her nerves and then fly into a rage when Julia would respond with a look of patient indulgence, as if she were merely humoring him. The fights seemed to come out of nowhere, like rats suddenly tumbling out of the ceiling—irrational, absurd.

Raúl had planned to build the house out of wattle and daub, a cheap, beautiful material that's easy to work with, but in the end it was built of unstuccoed adobe, Julia's idea—and it was also her idea to have all the corners rounded. Good ideas, both of them, since adobe is more durable and the soil there has a lot of clay in it. They made the adobe bricks themselves and the house didn't end up costing much. Adobe is a gentle color and it highlights any woodwork. The house has no right angles. They brought in a master builder from Villa de Leiva, a craftsman, really, whom Raúl was familiar with because he'd come across his adobe work in a book— projects he'd designed himself, a kind of rustic Gaudí, gorgeous stuff. Incredibly quiet and gruff looking, Segundo was, like a mule, and unquestionably a genius. And grumpy as all get-out. He was quick to anger, like Nosferatu from the Zen center, but his results were more visible, because he created beautiful things, unlike the Zen master, who doesn't produce particularly tangible results, in Raúl's opinion, since as far as he can tell, the people who go to him seeking his guidance leave, months or even years later, as mixed up as when they arrived. And possibly missing some blood. Or with weaker blood, anyway, since the food's pretty meager there. The disgruntled participants say the teacher tries to rip the self out with a stick.

Segundo completed the fireplace according to his own whims. Raúl left him instructions, and when he came back the crafts-man had done something that was phenomenal, sure, but totally different from Raúl's notes. But the fireplace came out so nice that Raúl couldn't even get mad. Segundo had acquired a huge slab of stone from somewhere and set it on top of the cubby for storing firewood, it stuck out so you could sit on it while lighting the fireplace. It looked like one of those mud ovens for baking bread. It was framed by abstract decorations formed from mud that had been smoothed until it was almost the texture of wood; the decorations were spiky or rounded, but discreet, and the chimney rose in faint curves that gave the sense it was made of living matter.

Gaudí himself would have sat down to gape at it.

A real piece of work. If he agreed with Raúl's instructions, he'd follow them to the letter, but if he preferred his own vision, there was no human power that could stop him from doing things his way, like with the fireplace. Between his incredible skill and his incredible obstinacy, Raúl had no choice but to simply trust that everything would turn out fine. And everything always turned out better than fine. When they publish photos of his house, he'll request that they give credit to Segundo, which will make the man very happy, but Raúl swears he'll never work with him again; Segundo's stubbornness had worn him out by the end of every project.

All these years in this business have made Raúl an expert in master builders.

It smells like ripe plantain cake with guayaba syrup. No, it smells like chicken marsala.

Braulio, the builder who helped him with Julia's house, never got used to Raúl treating him like an equal, and by the end he started getting cocky even though he had only mediocre skills—Raúl had to fire him for his disrespect. And flyspeck William, the builder he's working with these days, commits egregious mistakes and tries to convince him that everything looks great, that Raúl's just looking at it wrong. In the house they're building right now on the outskirts of Zipacón, William claimed the electrical outlets weren't actually installed crooked: it was an optical illusion, he said, from the way the light was falling on them. "Illusion, my ass," Raúl told him. The client laughed. She was beautiful. A foreigner. French. Not so young. Raúl made him take them out, and the second time they were how they were supposed to be. He's a nice guy, William is, entertaining as a monkey, but you can't work like that and Raúl's going to have to look for somebody else. Julia never met him. She would have detested him.

Rather than respecting Segundo, Julia feared him, though she never would have admitted it—she couldn't stand being afraid. She found it humiliating. The day she met Raquel, Raúl could tell she was trying hard not to show panic. She was beautiful, yes—small, with her head held high and defiant like a little terrier. She gave Raquel an effusive hug that threw her off. Later, talking about her cat and her great love for it—or neurotic obsession, really—Julia became the ten-year-old girl, which threw Raquel off even more.

For those six long months, Segundo and Julia avoided each other. Whenever Raúl and Segundo talked construction, she'd listen closely but wouldn't say anything. Afterward she'd offer her comments to Raúl and tell him what he needed to relay to the builder. From the beginning, Raúl knew she might leave him at any moment, but he continued making plans as if they would stay together all the same. Her restlessness, which she at first refused to acknowledge, much less articulate, had started gnawing at his spirit back in the Botanic Garden days. He became more and more cautious in everything he said and did. And she and Raúl could have gone on that way for a long time, decades, or till the end of their days, even, with him being careful not to provoke her, weighing each word, and her always on the verge of getting fed up and splitting.

The problem was the poems.

It is impossible to veil boredom. Better to have a heart attack, Raúl thinks, or for the world to end once and for all, than be forced to listen to a poem or give his opinion on it. But Julia, even seeing his expression, insisted—proud, imperious. Raúl used to tell her he didn't know anything about poetry, he was more into crime novels, and she, curt and enraged, would retort, "Poetry isn't written for people who know poetry. It's written for everybody."

Why didn't she dedicate herself to singing instead, or advertising? That was what she was really good at. Maybe then they would have been happy.

Raquel

She's been in Saskatoon for more than forty years, Adela has. Unbelievable. Summers ten days long, winters where it gets down to seventy below. Compared to that, Inwood is practically a tropical paradise—might as well be on the banks of the Magdalena River. Alberto, Lucía, and Marta have never left Colombia. Marta has barely been out of Teusaquillo, and Alberto, Raquel thinks, hardly leaves his house. Only to go into the office, which is two blocks away, and then back home again. Unmarried siblings keeping each other company. Lucía has done some traveling, but nothing extensive. When Raquel visits the house, she feels like her mother is there, reading or weaving in her room. Of the five of them, Raquel is the only one who's been to Raúl's ranch. Were the plains of Abraham in Saskatoon? Good reading for teenagers. Internet search. Sherwood Anderson? No. The novel takes place in Canada—Raquel read it as a child. Raúl has his father's library, all of it, meticulously maintained, including *The Plains of Abraham*, but it's going to rot on him because the place is so damn humid. The night she first visited Raúl's ranch, there was enough rain and fog to make you cry. Rain, fog, streams, springs, rushing ravines . . . Too much. The air is perpetually saturated. Everything seeps and drips—you have to wear rubber boots all the time, and you can never tell if it's hot or cold. The vegetation is amazing, for sure, but Raquel thinks the countryside is crap, especially the damp region where Raúl lives. Out there in the middle of nowhere, in nature, a person could die of melancholy. "A ridiculous place where the hens fly around uncooked," George Bernard Shaw called it. Her mother hardly ever visited the property her father bought in Pacho, which was a bust financially—everybody but Raúl was better with that stuff than her. And he's extravagant in other ways. Making Julián chicken noodle soup. Raquel doesn't want him to quit drinking, but he could practice some moderation at least, though moderation is completely foreign to him—in sex, thank God, and in everything else too. At eleven he'll wake up, eat some soup, have a few shots of whiskey, and go back to sleep at around three or even later, with *Leaves of Grass* splayed on his belly again. Raquel doesn't get women who agree to be with a man and then

98

want to change him. Raúl has always addressed people using a mix of "usted" and "vos," the standard formal and regional informal for "you," which was the unschooled way they talked at home, and suddenly here he comes using nothing but "tú," the standard informal, because Julia demanded it. She used to correct him in public. "*Usted?*" she'd ask. The old biddy.

And she made him wear brightly colored sweaters, when he likes gray and black.

"You look like a brown-skinned golfer. Or a fat caddie, more like," Raquel used to tell him. Raúl would grin.

"Sturdy," he'd correct her. "Glad you like the sweater."

Her little brother is big in every way, Raquel thinks. Big body, big heart. To make his ill-tempered, beloved little monkey happy, he said "tú" and wore red and yellow costumes.

Julia

I feel sorry for my father. His daughter has become water and air, and he refuses to accept it. He always travels anywhere people claim to have seen me. He doesn't sleep well. He dreams I show up at his house and knock on the door, but it's as if he's trapped in his bed, and eventually I get tired of waiting and leave again. My brothers look after him; though he's strong and lucid, he's an old man now. But his sadness is vast, and they can't help him with that.

He misses his only daughter.

For a poem: "Everyone is alone with their own sadness."

My poetry was as sensitive to sadness as it was to joy. In the book I dedicated to Raúl, or the one I wrote thinking of him, rather, since my father was the only person to whom I explicitly dedicated any of my writing—a poem, not even an entire book—joy is very present. That book of love was born out of our first months on the ranch, while we were building his house, when I was so happy. But his response was not remotely what I'd expected. His detachment, his scrupulous politeness, wounded me to the core, because I realized the poems hadn't moved him, hadn't interested him, and the couple of comments he'd made had been made out of obligation. He wasn't loquacious, it's true—he was pathologically quiet, in fact—and he wasn't a reader of poetry, as he explained to me several times, too many times that day, but even so I was despondent. It broke me in two, as I told him afterward. It was published in *Lunatic Moon*—not a well-known journal, but very high quality—and I got excellent feedback from my blog friends.

I had to practice a lot of patience and tolerance with Raúl because he was such an odd duck, with that tendency he had of not wanting to be seen, wanting to disappear, to evaporate—the kind of person who could have shone brighter but for some reason refused. If it was out of bashfulness, I have to admit I found it pathetic in someone who was no longer young, like him, who'd turned fifty-five six months after we came back to Colombia. Bashfulness is ridiculous in the elderly. But he was passionate and enormously caring, which I missed, especially once I was married to Humberto, who turned out to be so brutal, so cruel.

And the house turned out gorgeous. I wrote a poem describing my impressions of it, but I didn't want to show it to Raúl because by then I was beginning to see that he wasn't going to be interested in my things. Which is to say, my world, my life. Given the way he'd reacted to the love poems, after all! It's fine. Maybe I'm not a great poet . . . Of course, nobody knows that; only the centuries can decide; the matter no longer concerns me. But it wasn't about that. My passion for words was genuine, my love for them enormous, and he wasn't able to see that or understand it. And so one day I wrenched myself out of his life and shredded it to the bone.

They've looked for me through mountains and jungles. They've asked after me in dodgy neighborhoods in cities I've never visited. They've even searched for me here, where I no longer am. But they haven't seen me. Is it that I don't want to be found? What day is it today in that place where there are still dates? Do I not want them to realize I no longer have a way to put on my earrings? Helicopters have flown over the places where I no longer am and those where I have never been. My brothers tell my father that they're going to keep searching for me. What for?

My daughters, on the other hand, occasionally forget about me. People thought I'd left Raúl suddenly, but that wasn't so. I did rip him apart, it's true, and with good reason. But before that there was a decay slower than the one produced by water beneath the reeds.

Raúl

The woodstove is beautiful with its pinkish copper fittings, which Sonia keeps polished to a high shine. The gas stove seems to be just in case. Segundo did a phenomenal job here too, with his colorful mosaics made of broken tiles, designs that he created on the fly as he installed them. Sonia prefers cooking certain dishes on the woodstove. Chicken sancocho, for example. Cornmeal arepas. Who knows how long she'll be here with him; who knows what Raúl will do when she leaves. He is a loner who's never been alone. A bachelor who's always coupled up. But this time is going to be different, he thinks. Now he really is going to experience the big solitude, maybe, the final solitude, which will be added to the solitude of beginnings.

Life is a parade of people leaving—for another city, for another world, for the next world—and you stay behind, not really understanding why you haven't left too. Sonia seems happy, with her kitchen and her gardens, but she's a bit young to spend all her time in the countryside. Who knows if Raúl is even capable of being alone, especially now, with the memory of Julia. He'd have to ask for the apartment in Bogotá, go there from time to time to enjoy the company of the smoke and clamor and get drunk with his three remaining friends. Sonia can't get used to being kept, to not having her own money. Flight attendants make good money. It's brutal work. The air in planes is recycled, so when you travel, let's say to Paris, you spend eight hours breathing in the belches of the two hundred passengers on board.

The ground crew who open the plane doors when they land are blasted by a wave of halitosis, Sonia tells him, and have to hold their noses. Over time, flight attendants lose their memory because of the constant changes in pressure, Sonia says. Plus all the breathing in other people's gases, Raúl tells her, and especially because of the food. She laughs. She's got perfect teeth, Sonia does, a beautiful smile. Excellent hotels, excellent food in the hotels, horrible food on the airplanes, brutal schedules. When planes fly over the mountains, she stares up at them.

Not nostalgically, Raúl thinks.

Often, as he sits there, he seems to see Julia wearing her

flowered Mexican apron, walking toward him with a glass of rum on the rocks with lemon in each hand. She liked to cook and was good at it, though not as good as Sonia, who's a born chef. Her beef tongue with capers and tomato sauce is the best Raúl's ever tasted. Julia's presence in this house is looming and powerful. Her memory provokes sadness just as the presence of the dead does. In every block of adobe. In the tiniest details. In the big designs. When they were together, everything they experienced had an eternal quality to it, even if it lasted only the blink of an eye. During those months, the joy of being together, despite their fierce arguments, made them feel immensely durable, immensely stable. "You are the place where I am at home," Julia used to say. Julia and her clichés! Or "We're just passionate people," she'd say, referring to the intensity of their fights. The queen of pabulum, Raquel always called her. Did she really feel it? Raúl wonders. Was she really in love? Maybe perhaps who knows, as they used to say as kids. Well, and what's more clichéd than the fleetingness of things, the famous blink of an eye? As Raúl always said, "Why that sense of eternity in the drop of water hanging from the dry leaf suspended from a spiderweb barely clinging to the broken branch of a dead tree in the middle of the fog?" It may have been a cliché, but more elegantly garbed. They're clichés because they're true. *Exegesis of the Commonplaces* is

106

the title of one of the books he inherited from his father and has not yet read and will never read. Léon Bloy. Great name.

Raúl doesn't even know what exegesis means.

Boleros playing on the radio, on Tolima Stereo, as he sits on that same porch in that same chair that will be swallowed up by the earth. As they sipped their rum, Julia would sing boleros in the kitchen too, her voice full of warmth, and Raúl felt as if his heart were submerged in honey. She sang beautifully. The house was almost finished and they spent most of their time there. Segundo had left for the end the outdoor bathroom and the round pavilion built of bamboo and palm fronds with a stripey brazilwood floor, which Raúl hardly ever uses. Strung up in there is the hammock he and Julia bought a few days before the split—high-end, white, very expensive, fit for a Guajira princess—and that's where Sonia has been devouring the Russian novels. Raúl's the kind of person who hangs out on chairs on porches leaning back against the wall, not pavilions with fancy hammocks and stereo systems, tables, and glasses. A transistor radio at most.

Aleja

"I'm going to place the leftover lentils in the fridge, ma'am," Katerina says, and it pisses Aleja off. "Put, *put* the lentils, put!" she's almost on the verge of telling her, maybe yelling at her.

"Oh, do *place* them, Katerina, yes," she says instead, with all the venom she can muster.

The lentils came out delicious, with chorizo, but there was too much of it and leftovers turn tamasic. Eating chorizo once every thousand years doesn't do any harm. A vegetarian who eats chorizo, Humberto would tease. Or Katerina might say to her, "I'm so sorry, ma'am, how embarrassing, I wasn't applying my full attention." Ack! She could kill her. Would she talk to the homeless guy like that? Anyway, let that pig eat tamasic lentils. Aleja stuck a candle in a little cake she'd baked and opened a chilled bottle of white wine, but she didn't want to be by herself. She was feeling something—fear—so Katerina sat down with her. Aleja lit and blew out the candle and they ate as rain pattered on the dining room skylight and Katerina chattered about her mother's varicose ulcer that had finally been healed after many years. Though Julia was born at twenty minutes after midnight on January 10, Aleja celebrated her birthday a few hours earlier. She didn't want to say anything to Katerina, and the girl assumed it was Aleja's birthday. Calling Julia's brothers and father would have made her even sadder—they're gentlemen, all of them, and Aleja has very fond childhood memories of the father. She never heard anything about the mother again, nor had any interest in doing so. Aleja didn't like her much as a girl because she was quite mean to Aleja, and today she likes her even less. Let alone how mean the woman was to Julia. A yogi should avoid feeling affection or disaffection for things, should not discriminate with the mind, but Julia's mother is a special case. Horrible old woman. She always smelled of makeup. Aleja called the girls today. Diana didn't want to come to the phone, but Manuela did. They both cried.

They used to have wonderful birthday parties. Julia organized them herself. For Julia, Julia was always the most important person in the world. She hung up photos of herself in the library. Her father and Manuela were in second place, though a distant second, and neither of them got photos. She would start planning the parties far in advance, and sometimes they were themed. For her last birthday, the theme was the writer Doris Lessing, and she cooked the tomato soup that appears in one of her novels. Aleja isn't one for novels much, and even less for poetry. Julia used to see her reading her yoga and self-help books and sneer. "I'm a skeptic about that sort of thing," she'd say in a tone that made Aleja want to kill her. So it was almost better they didn't talk about books. Julia was snobby toward her . . . Raúl wasn't wild about literary parties either, or parties in general, really. Later, Julia started hosting these literary evenings where several poets would read their work. Every Tuesday. Such a drag. Aleja went to a couple of them and didn't get any of it. It was like they were writing so that people wouldn't understand. They congratulated each other. Julia didn't bother asking Aleja if she liked her poems. She considered her hopeless in that arena and was indifferent to her opinion. And she was right, Aleja thinks. The last poem Aleja read was a nursery rhyme. Of course, the *Tao Te Ching* is poetry too. The two of them were childhood friends, way before she became a writer, and Aleja still doesn't understand why she loved Julia like a sister. Or hated her like a sister, rather. Those kinds of things a person never understands, especially when they begin during childhood. They just happen, full stop. No helping it. The literary salons took place at the apartment in Bogotá, and maybe that's why Raúl stopped going and holed up at the ranch instead. That isolation of his had a lot to do with Julia's decision to leave him, Aleja thinks. "He didn't share my world," Julia told her one day, as an apology, because she knew Aleja hadn't agreed with how Julia had done things. Not what she'd done, but the painful way she'd done it. "You've always found excuses to stop loving people," Aleja replied, to take her down a peg—and to stand up for Raúl a little, frankly. They'd had plenty of fights since they were kids. Julia didn't reply, but she didn't speak to her for almost a month and Aleja knew full well why she was so angry. At least she didn't tell her that time not to stick her nose in other people's business.

Raquel

Sometimes the smell of the broth wakes Julián up, but he's had a lot to drink this time, and over a short period of time, so even the angel sounding the trumpet at the Last Judgment wouldn't rouse him. He's sprawled dead in the hammock, except he's breathing. Hopefully he'll go to bed without drinking any more. If she gives him some broth, he barely opens his eyes and then passes out again. She puts in a lot of cilantro, to act as a narcotic.

Every time she walks past the fire escape and sees the foamy layer of snow, she thinks of Julia. That mind of hers! You don't mess around with a person's head, Julián, who knows her, is always saying. Now I'm going to start feeling sorry for her—what about my problems? thinks Raquel. Death is crap, but it isn't the worst thing; this is. And in Colombia the papers are still obsessed with the story. Photos of that daddy's boy, all handsome, mocking, like he's saying, "Prove I did something to her, go on, if you're so smart." An arrogant look on his face, just like O. J. Simpson or like that preppy guy who strangled his girlfriend one night in Central Park, behind the Met. What was his name? Her last name was Levin. Preppies, the two of them. She was petite, and he was a big guy. He said she'd tied him up and things had gotten too rough during a sex game, and he'd accidentally killed her trying to get her off of him. "I've been in this line of work a long time," the judge said. "And as far as I know, you're the first man to have been raped by a woman in Central Park." After this joke, the judge tossed him in prison, and the bastard had a rough time of it in there.

There was even a search warrant issued for Raúl's house, who knows by whom, some judge, but the two police officers just drank coffee out on the porch. As far as searching went, they didn't search a thing. A few days later it was the anti-kidnapping unit, and they nosed around a bit more, but barely. They're too busy going after El Mono Jojoy, the guerrilla fighter, to waste their time on Raúl. He's a nasty guy, El Mono, Raquel thinks. Not a revolutionary bone in his body. As long as there's no ransom note, there's nothing they can do. He's got peaceful eyes, Raúl does, like a yogi, a saint. Like a big puppy dog. But he is strong. He could have drowned her hardly lifting a finger, or just put a pillow over her face and been done with it. A few little scratches on his arms. Like strangling a kitten. Why does Raquel always come up with these awful images? So many murders that never saw justice. So many blackened or gouged-out eyes, knocked-out teeth, split lips, broken bones, organ injuries, concussions. Women left paraplegic, with just one eye, with missing ears, no teeth, hobbling, braindead, deceased . . . Not to mention the endless anguish, the torment of irremediable sadness. They're brutes, men are. Raquel should take the opportunity to give the guy in the hammock a kick in the ass, and when he wakes up with a start, tell him it's for the women in Ciudad Juárez. If he wakes up. Just kidding. Poor guy. How could she think such a thing! With how gentle he is. Her sisters tell her she should be careful not to be too hard on him with the crap she says sometimes.

Raúl

When they're on the porch or on the upstairs balcony at night and a jet passes by high above, lit up like a firefly, Raúl says to Sonia, "There go your coworkers, breathing passenger farts." She looks at him with a mix of horror and disgust, and doesn't laugh. "Passenger wind," Raúl corrects himself, and with that he succeeds in wresting a chuckle out of her. Sonia just read *The Death of Ivan Ilyich*, and found it moving. He likes Tolstoy too, though he hasn't exactly been a dedicated reader. It's the same thing with books as with movies: he can't help seeing the somersaults they're performing to suck people in, and as soon as a writer pulls their first trick, he loses interest in the book. Everything's a trick with these things. The wall isn't smooth and beautiful; inside it's made of dung, clay, grass, and bamboo fibers. The house of the Lord is built of garbage and manure. But there are fake tricks and then there are real tricks.

It's one thing to build the house of the Lord and another thing to just be after money. Whereas Sonia goes from Tolstoy to the clumsiest bestseller without missing a beat. "The book isn't any good, but I can't stop reading," she'll say. Raúl tried to explain about fake tricks and real ones and he saw Sonia's attention starting to depart from her body, like it was trying to take off to heaven. And now Raúl's starting to feel hungry for real. Sonia doesn't care about tricks. "And she's right, I'm a pain in the ass." The best chicken marsala he ever had was in that club in Bogotá the one time he went there with Julia and her parents. That was where he first encountered the dish. He'd mentioned it to Sonia and eight days later they had it on the table. Who knows where she got the wine. The recipe was from the internet. And it came out almost as good as the club's.

If it weren't for her depressive spells, Sonia would be a perfectly happy person. They come on all of a sudden, like being hit by a brick, and vanish just as suddenly, as if they'd never happened and she'd been uninterruptedly happy since childhood. She locks herself away and doesn't talk. The light in her eyes goes out. "They turn straw-colored. I look like a charred chicken," she says. She lies down—to sleep, Raúl assumes—not in their bed, but instead shuts herself up in one of the other bedrooms. Sometimes he knocks on the door to make sure she hasn't hanged herself from one of the oak beams. That's how vicious the onslaught of sadness is. "I'm still here, Raúl, don't worry," she says in a neutral voice, a voice neither weak nor powerful. They talk about consulting some kind of physician or psychiatrist, but they never do. She gets better and they drop it. They've been lucky now that all of this with Julia happened—it's been months since Sonia suffered a depressive episode. And she's at peace with all of it, much more than Raúl is.

Raúl sometimes feels like Julia is watching them from somewhere. He mentioned it to Sonia and she said the same thing had happened to her after the death of her eldest brother. No way he's mentioning it to Raquel—she'd freak. Yesterday, when they were texting, she told Raúl she feels like Julia isn't dead, like she might have been turned into a zombie or something, somewhere out there. What's that supposed to mean? Raúl asked. They gave her something, scopolamine or something, they spiked her drink with burundanga and accidentally overdid it or something, she wrote. And after a moment she added, "Anyway, she was pretty braindead already." She makes dark jokes to disguise how much this whole business has affected her. She surprised him with that one.

Julia

What I miss most is the forms of things. Now that I don't have them, I understand them; I would be capable of writing like the gods. But there are no hands anymore. Now, finally, everything is complete and I no longer have to struggle to see the hidden face of anything. Before, I used to see surfaces, husks, appearances. I miss all of that. Before, I would see a mountain that was dark blue in one area, green in another, and I couldn't figure out where the blue ended and the green began. That's what made it so beautiful. Not anymore. I now know that blue does not exist and green does not exist. Everything is circular now. Everything is complete. Cold. Stiff.

I am not here, and yet I am cold. It's as if I were there, where the snow is piling up. Or out in the elements, standing among the irises, or in the bamboo at Raúl's house, in front of the house, shivering in the rain. Everything is a gelid dream. The house came out stunning. Many things were done as I suggested. My spirit was in them and dwells in them still, but I grew increasingly fed up with how little interest he took in my world, and I needed to seek out another future in which I'd be valued for who I was, in which my work, my passion, my life would be appreciated. And it looked so beautiful from the porch, the bamboo in the rain! I wrote a poem: "Rain on Bamboo." Raúl had designed a grove on the left side of the house—a big one, five hundred meters square, maybe more—and he'd left a clearing in the middle, reached by a winding path through the bamboo, and in the clearing he'd placed several boulders where you could sit in silence and feel the denseness surrounding you. He was unique, an artist in his way. And I had to murder that porch, and that bamboo, and those reeds, and that beautiful kitchen we built, and our bedroom, and the furniture. All murdered. And murder him too, so that I could be myself.

If it were me, I'd feel sleepy after what happened. I'd want to fall asleep forever.

Aleja

Katerina went to bed and Aleja was alone. She placed herself in the bed, Katerina did. If Aleja went to bed at ten like her, she'd fall asleep, sure, and then at midnight she'd be wide awake, blazing like a light bulb. She could call Humberto, but he'd realize that she's missing him, and that's no good. If anything comes up and in three months he can't pay her the thirty million pesos they agreed on, Aleja will have to delay opening the Santa Bárbara location. No thinking about that now. Julia never would have lent him the money. She once overheard them having a nasty fight about money, and Humberto was right: Julia was stingy. Tight-fisted ever since she was a kid. She even refused to lend Aleja the paltry five million pesos she urgently needed for an apartment, and Aleja ended up not being able to buy it. Julia didn't have the money just then, she said. Of course she did. Whereas Aleja has to be careful not to go splashing money around like an idiot. That's why she always liked Raúl—he's generous, not grasping. Money comes to Aleja effortlessly, but it goes just as readily. She invests it quickly, in real estate, before it turns into pocket money, and then rents out the properties, leaving them in the hands of a property manager. For yogis, money is not bad or good in and of itself. It is a flow of energy, like prana. Real estate isn't the most profitable, but you get to hold on to your capital and make a little money. Julia wasn't generous, but she was loyal, and she was always there for her when things were hard. The few times Aleja got sick, she was there. She kept tabs on her when Aleja's father was sick for so long. She was a good friend, ever since they were kids, even if she was bossy. Up until she was about seven, she looked like a child movie star or a little girl from the royal family of Monaco. Her mother used to dress her up to show her off to her friends. She could have been in *¡Hola!* magazine. Her father always had her sing for visitors, or in the club, and his eyes would glow watching her. Julia told Aleja once that her mother hadn't loved her because she was jealous of her father's affection. Julia's mother was one of those women who adores men and hates all women. And she'll keep wearing makeup till she's got one foot in the grave, Aleja muses. Then Julia started wearing jeans and playing soccer or flying kites with her brother in the parks, or playing tennis and golf at the club with her father. She didn't want to wear prissy dresses anymore, and her mother hated her even more for hopping from activity to activity. People would think she was a tomboy, she told her.

On the 24th of January, Humberto is supposed to make the first interest payment.

Raúl

Sonia cleans the kitchen till it gleams and goes off to the hammock to read until midnight. Once she's plowed through the whole library, they'll have to go out and buy a couple of cubic meters of books from one of the used bookstores in Bogotá. Like a sponge: it all gets stored on her hard drive. First cigarette of the day at ten p.m., not bad. Five a day, and a year ago Raúl was smoking ten. At first Julia found it weird how he would sit out there in the dark and smoke. Raúl once explained, almost apologetically, that it allowed him to see the little lights of the fireflies and the airplanes more intensely. Night after night after night until midnight. And he's up at four in the morning, since he's one of those people who don't need much sleep. According to Julia, the fact that his days and nights followed a nearly identical pattern week after week, month after month, indicated mental rigidity, spiritual atherosclerosis.

He was anal-retentive, while she was a free spirit who might go to bed at ten or eleven or midnight, who knew. A real wild thing!

The day the work on the house finished, they got into a huge fight.

To celebrate, he and Julia had gone up to drink rum on the second-floor balcony at sunset. They were thrilled that Segundo and his assistant weren't going to be showing up at seven a.m. the next day, with the assistant whistling to beat the band and Segundo working like a madman, scowling silently. Work is like a drug for Segundo. If he couldn't resolve construction problems, design buildings, set bricks, spread stucco, he'd have to be sedated and bundled into a straitjacket. That's the trouble with geniuses. He works at a good clip and is organized. And he never stops. At six in the evening he takes off without saying goodbye and goes to gets drunk on beer in the nearest shop. The next morning, still wobbly from the hangover, he plunges back into the day's work word-lessly—joyfully, Raúl would posit, though there's no way of know-ing. The hangover fades quickly. The assistant whistles constantly, probably to combat the silence, and occasionally says something to which Segundo, focused on his work, does not respond.

Raúl would have a hard time reproducing the fights he and Julia had in any detail, they were so ridiculous. The topic of ex-husbands set them off the night the construction of the house was complete. Raúl doesn't know why Julia suddenly decided to tell him what life with each of them had been like. He hadn't asked and didn't want to know about her extensive romantic life. He wasn't interested in knowing how decent her first husband had been, and he had to muster a great deal of patience to listen to her describe how she had sometimes found his tremendous decency incredibly dull, but that it had been his grouchy personality that had ultimately prompted her decision to end the marriage. She continued with number two. An artist. A painter. Raúl's eyes in the darkness of the balcony were filling with tears of boredom, and his heart with an overpowering unease. "Why is she telling me all this?" he wondered. Of her second husband, Julia said that he'd eventually inspired a kind of frigidity that verged on physical revulsion. Raúl stopped listening. Julia wasn't done with the second yet, and there were two to go. There was Diego, the talented and handsome photographer who was missing an eye. And there was the nationally renowned artist who'd left her and whose leaving had wounded her "to the ends of the earth." Raúl doesn't remember his name. There was a lot left to get through. Christ.

An awful fight. Raúl doesn't remember exactly what he said to Julia, though he can guess. "I don't give a flying fart about your past lovers," he would have said, but maybe he said flying fuck instead. Julia had stormed out of his house. Afterward Raúl learned she hadn't gone back to her place but instead had been driving, alone at that hour of the night, to calm herself down, and she'd ended up taking a little-known, longer route to Bogotá. When she was tense, she used to go out driving around aimlessly. Her father had taught her to drive when she was just a girl; she was a fantastic driver. Raúl isn't a good driver and could appreciate her skill. Julia often used to run off to villages in Boyacá, which she loved, and would spend the night in inns or hotels or in houses of families who took her in.

Humberto Fajardo told the police that was precisely what she'd done after an argument they had over the phone, with him in Bogotá and her out on her ranch. When she was driving like that, she could easily travel as far as the Eastern Plains, hours away, and she'd once ended up in a hotel in Cartagena after driving twenty-four hours straight, blasting music and occasionally weeping. Manuela said her mother never reached her apartment in Bogotá, where she was supposed to stop before meeting up with Diana at a shopping center. Diana claims she never showed up. And since they took so long finding her SUV, it was believed she'd disappeared with it.

Julia

If I hadn't been outmatched in sheer brute strength, I would never have let anyone take me down. I would have clawed and bitten my way free. I would have gouged out those eyes. No one was ever able to handle me. It's best if nothing's ever found, so my father doesn't have to see me humiliated and all dismembered by someone who turned out to be a ferocious wolf in gentle lamb's clothing. Poor Diana, who didn't know what she was doing. Poor Manuela. And now there is only this fog, thanks to which finally I understand everything, but only when I am no longer me—unable to write, unable even to sing. Poor, poor things.

My heart is disintegrating. My cheeks are coming undone. My eyes are becoming part of other creatures.

Raquel

The cilantro sent him straight to bed, as if he'd been hit over the head with a stick. He didn't even have time to brush his teeth. He's going to sleep less than two hours and then groggily get up to brush them and forget about the bottle of Gordon's. Ten thirty and here I am, lonely as the Anima Sola, Raquel thinks. The snow, at night, falling thickly past the window, is like the passage of time in a place somewhere outside of time, where, even though there is movement, everything remains unchanged. The passage of time when you are dead. Or drunk, like this turkey here. Or in a coma. Or braindead. Raúl is never online this time of night—only in the mornings and only for a short time. Raquel can't talk to him much about the images that come to her from who knows where, since Raúl doesn't put much stock in that witchy stuff, as he calls it, or her other intuitions. The night drags on and Raquel starts getting jumpy and nervous. But it isn't fear. It is, instead, as if she were able to see dark places that she would rather turn away from but always ends up looking at anyway. It's because of the snow, Raquel thinks, which is sometimes so sad and sometimes so beautiful.

Raúl no longer reacts when people talk to him about Julia. He tries to be kind and doesn't say anything, but he's obviously sick of the subject. Yesterday, by text, Raquel told him she was convinced Julia wasn't dead, and he lost it. "Where the hell is she, then? If she were a vegetable somewhere, they would have identified her. Don't you think?" Then he added, "Don't come at me with this shit now, Raquelita, all right? It's better if we don't talk about it."

His anger didn't surprise Raquel. First he's practically destroyed when Julia leaves him, and then what happened happened and everybody's buzzing with rumors and theories. Raquel gets that all Raúl wants now is to enjoy his young paramour in peace and his ranch, his bamboo, and he no longer gives a rat's ass what happened to the other woman. It's only natural that he doesn't want to keep hauling her around with him. But Raquel is annoyed by his snarls, no matter where they're coming from, and she won't let herself be intimidated by them. "It's not shit," she types, "it's a real possibility, Raúl, let's not kid ourselves." She'd heard of one woman, she went on, who'd been dosed with

129

scopolamine in Bogotá, taken to the Caribbean coast, and strangled, and her family members found her more than a month later in a morgue in Barranquilla. The corpse had been misidentified at first and stored in a fridge under another name, and they found her by pure chance. She could easily have never surfaced. To which Raúl replied that he had to go, the conversation was getting on his nerves and he had things to do. "Well go on, then, Mr. Ostrich, stick your little head in the sand if that's what you want to do," Raquel wrote.

They fought, really.

Still watching the snow through the window, Raquel sits down in the hammock on top of Julián's *Leaves of Grass*—he's always leaving things strewn around. She settles in, takes a deep breath to purge her annoyance, and places the book on her lap. Hammocks are so lovely! The cushion of snow on the steps is at least half a meter tall now. *Starting from fish-shape Paumanok where I was born, well-begotten, and rais'd by a perfect mother, after roaming many lands, lover of populous pavements . . .* So much light! So different from these caverns where we like to hole up. Not Raúl, no, he's a creature of the open air, and even when he gets violent, he's still innocent somehow, like a child. *There was never any more inception than there is now, nor any more youth or age than there is now, and will never be any more perfection than there is now, nor any more heaven or hell than there is now.* Wherever you read, beauty springs forth, like the water in Raúl's mountains, but there death and things more awful than death spring forth too. "The horror!" Kurtz said, in Marlon Brando's dusty-sounding voice. Addressing the topic in class. Coppola. Conrad. She's a happy person, Raquel is, but she knows awful things, to her dismay, and death too.

She has an ear for them and for music.

Raúl

They made up after the fight provoked by Julia's droning on about her four husbands, but things seemed to deteriorate rapidly. Julia spent all day writing, which worried Raúl; he knew that the avalanche of creativity would sweep them toward disaster. And he had to conceal how silly he found her writerly airs: the gaze probing the clouds for profound truths, the furrowed brow of the impassioned poet, the photos of herself on the walls, on the book-shelves. Terribly serious. Always striking.

He began to be afraid.

One day Raúl was in Julia's apartment in Bogotá and a bunch of poets suddenly showed up: three young women, practically little girls, along with a smooth-faced, obese young man and a woman on the cusp of old age, who had a raspy voice, chain smoked, and gave the impression of having been an alcoholic up until very recently.

They all pulled out their notebooks. The almost elderly poet drew a flask of rum out of her purse, fetched some drinking glasses, and suddenly he was out of place in the room. Things got even worse when the poets began to read their work aloud. The young women eyed him as if he were an intruder. The poems were impenetrable. He went to the bedroom to toss his belongings into a backpack and left the apartment, barely saying goodbye. He went back to the ranch. After a while he even felt some degree of relief—apprehensive relief, if you can call it that—because he felt certain the tensions were going to explode, the misunderstanding would be cleared up, and the two of them would split.

That night, almost without thinking, he called her and told her he wanted to end the relationship. She expressed surprise and objected. She did not cry. She said she was sad they were breaking up before their relationship had given everything it had to give. Raúl told her to leave a suitcase with the doorman with the few things of his that were in the apartment, and he'd come by for them. Julia's voice turned metallic, very tense. She was furious. Raúl will never know for certain, but he thinks it caught her off guard that he was the one breaking up with her. Playing amateur psychologist, he thinks her mother broke up with her too many times when she was a little girl; having found the experience unbearable, she simply refused to allow it to happen again. She told Raúl she would return his things when she was good and ready. "Keep them, then," he replied. "It's junk anyway."

Aleja

Katerina is snoring. So young and so fancy-talking, and yet she snores. The problem is the way her trachea is shaped. Aleja never snores. Yoga keeps us free of many defects and afflictions, and its effects are immediate. Half an hour of poses, and the melancholy generated by the blowing out of Julia's candle evaporated as if by magic. For Tarot, the hour at which a person was born is vitally important. When Julia and Aleja tried to find out the time of Julia's birth, it was her father who gave them the information, not her mother. Her mother had said it was better to forget terrible things, and then, pretending to correct herself, added that she was referring to the pain of childbirth, naturally, not to the fact that Julia had come into this world at all, which had delighted everyone, had it not? Evil old crone. And she laughed. Aleja wished the debit card thieves had put a little more effort into it and left her crippled or something. With just one eye, for example, so she had to do her makeup around the patch. Breathe deeply until all rancor, all hate leaves the body. Yogis have all of the human passions—they're just capable of keeping them under control. Ugly business!

Aleja thinks a cup of green tea will balance her. Quite a downpour out there. Listen to Katerín go! She sounds like the electric pumps on Aleja's dad's ranch in Mariquita, when they used to irrigate the sorghum crops. He'd loved his ranches so much, but nasty accusations landed him in house arrest. A year of house arrest, and by then his heart was weakened by grief and he was ready to die. He'd been a scapegoat for the many, many enemies he'd made when he was involved in politics. They're trying to do the same thing to Humberto—but he's not letting them. He's no fool. Six months dragging that oxygen tank around, Aleja's dad, and dragging sadness around which never let up. Julia was very kind to him—an odd alliance, as Julia was not exactly known for her generosity. But she had asthma and understood.

Sometimes Aleja calls her Katerina, and sometimes Katerín, and she doesn't actually know what her real name is. The girl has told her like forty times, and Aleja's too embarrassed to ask again. Green tea is rich in antioxidants. They're all going to end up oxidizing in this damp air, Aleja thinks, if it doesn't stop raining. It's been the rainiest winter in decades, the national IDEAM office says. The photos in the newspaper are heartbreaking. All those people displaced, or drowned, all those swollen cows. Compassion is the most notable trait of the enlightened human being, and detachment is second. That doesn't mean you cut all ties with the world of conventions. You have to respect conventions, but know what they are. Respect our commitments. If a person commits to something in monetary terms, they're supposed to come through.

Like with interest payments, for instance.

She once lent Humberto forty thousand pesos, and he still hasn't paid her back. But now we're talking about thirty million. You don't mess around with that.

Raúl

Raúl's belongings weren't junk. Julia had his camera, which wasn't bad. All of his "nice" clothes, the stuff he wore when giving lectures about vegetal steel, she had all of those, and there were a few garments—a leather jacket, for example—that Raúl was fond of. And books too, like the two volumes on the birds of Colombia and the complete works of an Italian poet, which Raquel had given him and which he enjoyed even though the poems were pretty much incomprehensible. In this regard, as in everything, there are two kinds of poets, Raúl the amateur critic opines: the ones who say hardly anything even though it seems like they're saying a lot, and the ones you know are saying a lot, but for whatever damn reason, they don't want you following along. Like that Italian guy. He should text Raquel and tell her his theory.

The camera, the leather jacket, the poet's complete works, neatly bound, and none of it got lost, not this time, because less than two weeks later, shattered by the hell of separation, which was like a rehearsal for the even more awful hell that would await him when eventually she left him, he called her to plead for them to get back together. Julia was back at her ranch. She didn't say they should see each other there or that she'd come to his, but instead decided that their reconciliation would take place on what she called "neutral ground"—a rural hotel in Villeta, three hours away—and she also decided they wouldn't travel together, but meet there instead. A torrid reconciliation, of an almost violent eroticism—clichéd, savage, right out of a movie. The hotel restaurant served wonderful food. "We ate and fucked like animals," as she put it. Afterward she wrote a poem in which she described the event in philosophico-erotic language. It got published.

The mist crept up onto the porch.

In mid-November, Sonia acquired a perfect pine tree, placed it on the porch, bought ornaments, decorated it, and now, just when Raúl was getting used to it and starting to enjoy the balls and lights, she started taking it down. He told her that Christmas trees got left up till Epiphany. She smiled and Raúl figured she was surprised he knew about Epiphany, since he's pretty out of it when it comes to that stuff. Sonia hung the ornaments again and plugged the lights back in.

"Epiphany was January 6th," she said.

It casts a beautiful glow there on the corner of the porch, especially when it's foggy, like right now.

Julia

My poetry was different from the rest of women's poetry, or erotic poetry, whether written by men or women, in that I didn't lose my head when I was writing; I never got carried away with sensuality, so I never failed to be profound. If somebody didn't understand the concepts and intuitions I laid out in a poem, too bad for them. Profundity isn't for everybody. What is it that we find in profundity? Mud. Mud of a sort that makes it indistinguishable from everything else, so everything else turns to mud as well. Viscous, suffocating. Like a hammock. Good thing I can't feel it anymore!

In Villeta, I drove Raúl mad with love. They published my poem in a Medellín poetry journal with national distribution. When I used to read it at readings and festivals, people would clap for a long time. Of course that also had to do with how striking I always was, even if I didn't feel beautiful. Talent and physical attractiveness aren't necessarily linked—quite the opposite. I miss that—the applause, the heat of in-person readings. Eroticism, like death, allows you to touch the beyond. It isn't the same reading a poem silently as reciting it aloud. Being dead isn't the same. At bottom, there is only silence.

My father was told I was in Antigua, living under an assumed name, and the poor man got on a plane and went looking for me. But how could he have found me when I haven't budged from this place where I am and yet no longer am? How is it possible that I can't even see the fog?

Our reunion was beautiful. I spent it in the swimming pool. Happy. The past is so gorgeous! How wonderful if I were able to remember it now! We made love, played ping-pong, swam, ate, made love again. Something was telling me that our renewed connection wasn't going to last. Raúl even pretended to take an interest in my writing projects and my Wednesday night salons. Humberto was better able to appreciate me than Raúl, though of course his foul temper made him callous, and greed, when he wasn't earning as much as he'd hoped, made his foul temper even worse.

Raquel

We don't know anything about this world, Raquel thinks. Whitman says so too. *A child said What is the grass? fetching it to me with full hands. How could I answer the child? I do not know what it is any more than he.* But then Whitman starts talking about what grass might be, and at that point, in Raquel's humble opinion, he fucks it all up. "The handkerchief of the Lord." "A scented gift." "The beautiful uncut hair of graves." Total fag, after all. He just freaking said he didn't know! He should have left it at that, not kept bumbling around with words. That's poetry for you. A flash of dazzlement and then blahblahblah. And it's not like this Borges guy is such a great translator anyway. He sounds stiff to Raquel, just like his poetry, if you look close. Half an hour, and the loveliness of hammocks turns to discomfort, and the discomfort to pain. Not even Neruda eludes the curse of the blahblahblah. A corpse rotting

143

in a hammock of mud. Raquel thinks she should take up drawing again, as a way to create an outlet for these images that come to her. Lift herself out of the mire of this hammock. People used to really like Raquel's paintings. And her rag sculptures too. Her dolls. She still makes them, but in her head, which isn't the same. She's too focused on her students. If she's not making dolls or drawings—actual ones, that is, not mental ones—she gets overwhelmed with images. She always did better when she grabbed some charcoal, or a wad of cotton, rags, and a needle.

Ever since she was a girl she's been leery of midnight. As it approaches, like right now, anxiety. Once she gets through it, relief. It's because of the stories the help used to tell when they were kids, back in Medellín. At the midnight hour, spirits in purgatory come out of the cemeteries to roam the streets in orderly, luminescent processions. Raquel can still see one image quite vividly in her mind's eye: a woman who sat sewing at her Singer, and, because she was reckless, something awful happened to her when the spirits passed by. She doesn't remember what. She'll have to ask Raúl. No. Alberto—he remembers even things that didn't happen. Such a fibber!

Up to the roof to look out at the lights of the bridges and the little boats on the Hudson. There will be a cushion of snow on the roof too. Doesn't matter if snow's still coming down, Raquel thinks. She'll put on a coat, hat, and boots and wait for midnight up there, admiring the river Walt Whitman admired.

Raúl

When they came back from Villeta, they went to Julia's apartment, not the ranch. They talked. Raúl promised to participate in her world more, since that was her biggest complaint: he didn't participate in her world. And "her world" didn't mean her daughters—Raúl was very fond of them—or her father, a total gentleman, or her brothers, who were good guys too, but the young-woman poets who were practically little girls, the alcoholic almost-elderly poet, and the fat young-man poet, and the other poets who sometimes came around, almost always very young, who admired her so deeply and who got on his nerves. Well, and it also meant her poetry.

Raúl thinks they should leave the Christmas tree and lights up all year. Being swathed in fog produces a mix of sadness and contentment akin to what he feels drinking aguardiente. Or felt, since he always eventually overcame the sadness and stopped drinking. Raúl gave Sonia a surprise on December 7, when he filled the whole place with paper lanterns. The porch, the two walnut trees out front, the bamboo grove. Like a dream. They disintegrated later that night, when there was a huge downpour. This time of day, Raúl starts feeling peckish again, and though there's leftover chicken and rice, he decides not to eat any more, since he's already too well fed. Juan Felipe told him not to worry, he didn't count as obese yet, and that night, terrified, Raúl dined on soda crackers with green tea. Obese! That young poet is obese. And what could he and Raúl, the two fatsos, possibly have to talk about, and what could he possibly talk about with the two arrogant young women? He's lucky to have Juan Felipe. Independent physician and even more independent Zen monk. Otherwise he'd have to go to the doctors at Seguro every time he had back pain or fight those same doctors to get them to prescribe him something strong for his insomnia. It comes in spells, the insomnia does. He's been sleeping a little better now that he's with Sonia, and he knows that when she leaves he'll stop sleeping altogether. Two months ago, Juan Felipe, fed up with Dracula's teaching methods, which he deemed medieval, called him an incompetent charlatan and left the monastery and the region altogether. Now if Raúl enters a long spell, he has to call up on the phone and wait for Juan Felipe to mail a prescription for Valium or whatever by post.

Sonia must be out there in the hammock, plowing through Thomas Mann. She's going to leave him soon, Raúl knows it. It's a big world out there, and he's fifty-four and quiet and solitary and a workaholic and not very good company, as Julia made clear in so many ways. This time he feels not blind anguish and panic, as he did when he found out Julia was leaving him, but a more philosophical fear. To be or not to be. Human beings are a tribe; they can't exist on their own—they die. Raúl doesn't regret anything he's said or done in life, even if it was harsh, but when you're on your own you tend to get all tangled up inside, and uneasiness and guilt inevitably rear their heads. That's what he fears. Good thing he has his work. And he'll always have the construction workers for company.

Tomorrow he'll be getting up early to deal with the saltcellar and start designing a Japanese deer-frightener, to be installed in the lake. Wells, people call lakes around here, regardless of how many water lilies they've got. The deer-frightener is for his personal enjoyment, since there's not a lot of commercial demand for them. *Onisho* or something like that, they're called in Japanese. He'll have to ask Sonia, who's got a memory like a Philips recorder. The

148

regular sound produced by the bamboo rapping against the stone is beautiful. The water moves the bamboo and the bamboo hits the stone. Thock! Pause, and again, thock! There needs to be some kind of sound to keep his impending lonely bachelor self company. He found several models on the internet, some of them far too complex. It would be good to install another one in the ravine.

No matter what he did, Julia would have left him. Raquel says she ate him up when she had a hankering and spat him out like a watermelon seed when she was done. "You're making me feel like a loser," Raúl protested. He couldn't tell her that he'd gotten his revenge anyway. "A loser and a half," Raquel said. "And that's putting it kindly." Who knows. Raquel hated her so much, maybe she was denigrating Julia despite herself, given how hard all of this has hit her. Really weird. All that's left is for Julia to come to her in a dream and tell her where she is. Heaven forbid! The icy lapping of fear runs up your spine and into your brain. With Raquel anything is possible. When she found out Raúl had crumbled and called Julia asking her to come back, she told him he was in for it now. "You'd better watch out for what's coming down the pike."

Aleja

The pumps on Aleja's father's ranch seem quiet compared to Katerina. Her snoring echoes through the entire apartment.

"Hey, Katerina, wake up, honey, you're suffocating! Turn over and maybe that'll stop it."

"Oh, so sorry, ma'am. How embarrassing!"

Her snoring had been moderate at first, but gradually picked up steam and ended up an earthquake. She'll tell Humberto. It'll make him laugh. Humberto's teeth are so straight, so white. Wonderful smile. He keeps a toothbrush and dental floss in his pocket and brushes them every time he smokes or eats anything. When he flosses, he's so meticulous that he looks like he's carving his teeth. Honing them, Raúl used to say—he never liked him much. That astronomical interest he'd insisted on paying her. Maybe a normal interest rate would have been better. Aleja had lost touch with Raúl after he and Julia split up. They didn't have anything in common, though they'd always gotten along. Aleja showed him a few asanas, which he'd pulled off nicely despite being overweight. He was more flexible than you'd guess. Julia had been the one to organize the get-togethers with the four of them at her ranch or her apartment, so she could have a social life outside of her poets, she used to say, and be able to include us, her best friends. Raúl has absolutely no social skills. The gatherings always started out tense, but things would loosen up as the wine flowed, and everybody would have a good time and laugh a lot in the end. Raúl can be pretty funny when he's a few glasses in, not to mention Humberto, with that sharp wit of his he's always dishing out. If you saw them together, you might almost think they were friends.

When Aleja found out that Julia and Raúl had gotten back together, she was happy but didn't harbor any illusions. She knew Julia well and could see the apathy in her eyes, even if she'd gone back to her old habit of perching on his lap. Julia later told her that Raúl was never able to enter her world and that's why she ultimately left him, but Aleja doesn't believe it. She was simply dying of boredom. In Aleja's opinion, Julia enjoyed the first part of relationships, the thrilling part, but eventually she wearied of her lovers and dumped them. Nor does Aleja believe that Raúl had anything to do with whatever has happened to Julia now, since even though he sometimes would fly into a rage, he's actually a placid guy. Kind of like an elephant—you've got to be gentle with them or they might get angry and even kill. Everybody who knew Julia has been questioned.

Raquel

Go up to the roof? Tea first. Since not everything is light and certain places that seem to beckon to her are not always peaceful, Raquel sometimes has a hard time making up her mind to go somewhere, and when she finally does, it's as astounding as she imagined, sometimes more so. Jasmine tea. That time she went out walking along the beach in Coney Island in the middle of an afternoon snowstorm, with an unruly, icy wind churning the foam on the waves. And the shifting subtleties of light that day—amazing! That beach is always magical, but you have to endure the hour-and-a-half subway ride from Inwood. When Raúl was really messed up over Julia, he used to go out there, even though it was high summer, as hot and swampy as tripe stew. Raquel even started thinking Raúl was going to end up staying to live there with the homeless under the boardwalk, or in one of the vacant lots, actually, since they don't let anybody stay under the boardwalks. They won't even let you set off firecrackers with the dragon, so they're definitely not going to let bums take a shit down there! "Get it through your heads. This is a city for the rich," the mayors say. But not even Giuliani could wreck New York. If September 11 couldn't take this city down, its mayors definitely won't be able to!

In her impatience, she's brewed the tea weak. *When I makes tea I makes tea, as old mother Grogan said. And when I makes water I makes water,* says Mulligan, from Joyce. Put the tea back on the stove, and this time let it steep. Almost impossible to teach *Ulysses* to kids from the inner city, even in an alternative school like hers. Maybe when they get to college. Sometimes she manages to get them to laugh a little, but she has to choose passages very carefully, make sure they get the joke. Raúl, who isn't the most sophisticated reader, liked the paragraphs she gave him to read. The end of "The Dead" is incredibly beautiful. A great poet, but especially in his prose, Raquel thinks. *Snow was general all over Ireland. It was falling softly upon the Bog of Allen and, further westwards, softly falling into the dark mutinous Shannon waves. It was falling too upon every part of the lonely churchyard where Michael Furey lay buried. It lay thickly drifted on the crooked crosses and headstones, on the spears of the little gate, on the barren thorns. His soul swooned slowly as he heard the snow falling faintly through the universe and faintly falling, like the descent of their last end, upon all the living and the dead.* And the sense of humor. One of the few times Raquel talked to Julia, she told her that Joyce had titled a book of poems *Chamber Music* and when he was asked to explain the title, he said it had occurred to him while he was listening to a maid pee in a chamber pot. Julia got really solemn, and Raquel realized that she'd mentioned it as a way to criticize how seriously poetry in general, and Julia's poetry in particular, took itself. She'd done so unconsciously, though not at all innocently, and Julia immediately caught what she was saying between the lines: "If Joyce, an incredible genius, could make fun of his own poetry, what's up with all your goofy transcendentalism?" Raúl says Julia was afraid of Raquel. If she was, she hid it well. She wasn't the first to be afraid of her, though, because when Raquel bites, she bites hard. And Julia had good reason to be afraid, seeing the sorry state she left Raúl in.

Julia

Given the opportunity to see anything again, I would choose to see reeds in fog. If I were granted that chance, that's what I would ask for. I wrote a poem once. When I was still able to gaze at fog and reeds and cliff and tree ferns on the cliff and algae. "Reeds and Fog," the poem was called. My blog friends really liked it. It came out in *Estravagario* magazine, but by that point I didn't have eyes to see it. The editor, Mercedes, praised me in an editor's note, but I had no way of knowing it. When Raúl and I had the big fight, he told me that my love for these mountains was a pose, an excuse to write "that poetry you write," he told me. He was irate and bellowing. "You'd be better off not writing anything than writing that crap." I was never anyone's doormat. If somebody yelled at me, I yelled back. If they hit me, I hit back. My love for the mountains was genuine.

Everybody looks at me and leaves, and that is because I'm no longer here. It's like they don't want to see me, and can't. It's like being in an aquarium where the light's burned out and with everyone all gathered around me. Like looking at everything in a time where my parents haven't yet been born. So sad, such overwhelming loneliness. But such peace here! Lovely.

Aleja

Apnea! thinks Aleja. That's what the poor girl's got. Sleep apnea. The motor-pump snoring is loud—and gradually grows louder, until at a certain point the pump jams and the sleeping beauty of the enchanted fairy wood awakes. She coughs or rolls onto her side, and since she's young, she promptly falls back asleep and soon rolls onto her back and the pump starts up again: inhale exhale loud louder louder still, choke, bam, wakes up, coughs, rolls over, falls asleep. There are yoga exercises for that, but Aleja doesn't know them. She'll google it. Nothing wrong with teaching the help yoga! The girl talks too fancy, never hears however hard she tries to listen. She's practically a child. Just twenty years old. Yesterday she told Aleja she used to play the mandolin with a little ensemble that plays Colombian music. She studied at Mono Núñez's music school for two years but couldn't afford to continue. Miracle she didn't say she was temporarily "illiquid." The human wastage in this country. Aleja can't stand so-called Colombian music, bambuco and that sort of thing, but that's a matter of taste, of course. Katerina should be studying, even if it is the mandolin, instead of squandering time in the kitchen and dealing with garbage and the homeless guy. One more slice of Julia's cake isn't going to make me fat, Aleja thinks. Katerina was lucky she ended up with her and not some old lady who would mistreat her like nobody's business. Aleja could train her in yoga so she can work in one of the academies in the chain Humberto's got planned. It's an idea. It's super profitable to work at a larger scale. Katerina's certainly not dumb—look how she handled the homeless guy. The challenge is going to be getting her to talk like a regular person. She even differentiates between her *b*'s and her *v*'s.

And listen to how clearly she enunciates when she's asleep.

Aleja made Julia's cake on Sunday, when Katerina wasn't around, using organic flour, and she recited the *Heart Sutra* as she prepared it. It vibed with Julia's image, her spirit. She set a photo of her on the kitchen counter while she mixed and chanted, and all of a sudden hail started clattering on the skylight. Aleja's not saying she . . . You never know. Organic sugar, eggs from bug-eating, free-range hens. Of course Julia must already know Humberto can't wait to rip off her panties. But what's it to her at this point! Besides, he hasn't got the widower look—or the inclinations! More of a player! If Aleja had let him that day, he would have pinned her against the living room wall like a butterfly. Yoga keeps us flexible, limber. Aleja must have ten years on Humberto, besides.

Raúl

One deer-frightener in the lake and another in the middle of the bamboo grove, taking advantage of how the little creek runs downhill. Their gentle knocking will alternate, as if each were responding to the other, and the sound will infuse the place with life.

Thock! — pause — Thock! says one in the falling rain.

Thock! — pause — Thock! replies the other.

The two detectives eyed all these trees and bushes as if they didn't get it. The lushness distracted them from what they'd come to ask. They said Raúl was living the way life was meant to be lived, but Raúl knew that within two days out here, the detectives would have been desperate to get back to the smoggy, treeless neighborhoods of Bogotá where they must live. One of them asked where the store was. "Far," Raúl said, emphatic. "And does it always rain like this?" the detective asked. "Often." It really gets city people down, makes them melancholy. It even gets Raúl down sometimes! Sonia brought them coffee and they asked Raúl if she was his daughter, though they knew full well she wasn't. Standard-issue cops. They asked about Humberto Fajardo. Raúl told them that as far as he knew, Humberto hadn't been out on Julia's ranch. He'd hardly been back since Julia went missing, he said. If Raúl's land made them uneasy, how would they feel at Julia's, with that cliff and that lake which conceal such doom and suffocation! The policemen asked out of obligation, without conviction, certain they'd never get to the bottom of anything and not really hoping to. Salaries and bribes were what they responded to, and they'd already received both. Third-world cops, at the end of the day, with a passel of children and not enough money for shoes and school supplies.

They'd found out about some things—you had to give them that. They knew about the fighting, for example, which had become more frequent and intense after the honeymoon in Villeta, but they mentioned it almost indifferently, as just one more negative fact that might inspire a bribe. When police pull people over on the highway, they bring up all the problems, anything that's unfavorable for the driver in any way: a broken turn signal, dirty windshield—almost unconsciously they build a case to ensure that a bribe is eventually offered. And people offer bribes because it's easiest, Raúl thinks, and thus chaos reigns in the nation.

The fights between Julia and Raúl were brutal—no denying that. He tried to hold back to keep life from becoming impossible, but eventually his mind generated only a perpetual monologue in which sarcasm was the prevailing tone, like a noxious mist, a morass. He was deeply in love with a person whom he did not respect. In response to all the mental cockroaches he claimed Julia was afflicted with, his mind offered a constant silent commentary: "Dotty old loon." Julia insisted on calling the tilapias in the lake "dolphins" as a poetic metaphor, and any time she said it, Raúl practically lost his mind. "Dotty old loon!" And she claimed to be a free spirit because some days she got up early and others late, whereas with him, even though he's attempted to play with time all his life, like a sort of watchmaker—or resembling a watch itself, really—he strove to be drinking his first cup of coffee by four thirty in the morning, at five on the dot he'd be reviewing the work completed the day before, at six sharp he'd be pouring a second cup of coffee, and at six thirty he would start wandering the coffee fields, looking at the trees and deciding on his work agenda for the day, an agenda that would follow the unchanging rhythmic patterns he embraced. Day after day after day. Sure, Raúl's little rituals are nonsense too, but they don't mean anything—they're just a game, and they don't hurt anyone or mean he's sclerotic.

And the ill will just kept building.

Raquel

"See?" Raquel said when Raúl told her how things were going. "What did I tell you? You started begging for forgiveness like a wimp instead of standing firm. *Don't weep like a woman for what you could not defend like a man.*"

He laughed and replied that though that old chestnut was a good one, it didn't entirely fit his situation, plus what choice did he have. After that Raquel stopped asking how things were going between them, because she knew, of course, and most of all because she didn't want to get overwhelmed with details. The details, as always, would arrive anyway, in dribs and drabs, through Alberto, who's a huge gossip, and everybody else, without her even asking.

It's gorgeous, all this snow. But sad.

Julia

He wasn't a literary critic, he said, but he'd offer his honest opinion of my poems anyway. He thought some of the poems in *Iris Flower* were just words arranged vertically on the page, and then, in an attempt to lessen the blow—typical condescending male—he told me he'd been able to feel the music in other poems, and I should keep working in that direction. The guy actually gave me advice! And he repeated several times that he wasn't a literary critic, as if that should take the sting out of his words.

So how did he expect me to react?

When I got that hard, indifferent response from him, something in me broke. From that point forward, I began to find Raúl's presence suffocating. I tried to put up with him, but it got harder and harder; it was wearing me out. I was thrilled whenever he went away; I'd get irritable when I learned he was coming back. I had created a beautiful book of poems, and I was legitimately happy and proud, since the endeavor had taken me an entire year. And then he comes along with a bucket of ice water! I told him, "You cracked me in two," but he went on as if he hadn't done or said anything. And even as our life went on with the same suffocating routines, Raúl was convinced the relationship was still solid. His routine-bound ways stifled my creativity. It was as if my arteries were calcifying.

The helicopters seem like they're flying between the raindrops, but you can't see or hear them. Anything we see and hear is always the product of our imagination.

It doesn't matter. It's probably somebody else they're searching for by now.

Raúl

Digging a little in the creek bed to make the change in elevation more pronounced so the bamboo deer-frightener raps the stone more loudly. If it weren't raining so hard, Raúl would get a flashlight and go have a look at the place where he was planning to install it. Ghost-frightener, really, since there haven't been any deer around here for centuries. Thock! Pause. Thock! to scare off Julia's specter, which won't leave him alone, to finally get it off his back.

The bamboo piece needs to be at least a meter long, and you slice one end on the diagonal so the water pours in better. The key is that the bamboo has to fill up enough to tip over from the weight. It's best to use a rounded stone so the opposite end of the bamboo makes a louder thock when it swings back down. *Shishi-odoshi*, Sonia says they're called in Japanese. "I do have a good memory," she says.

Raúl doesn't think Sonia will leave for good, either—he hopes not. Any moment now, he will see her get out of the taxi, a knock-out in her flight attendant uniform, in front of the house. The local taxis are total disasters from driving around on these torn-up roads. "Don't sit on that side, Doña Sonia. The roof's dripping from all this rain," the taxi driver will tell her. Sonia grew up in the countryside, and she likes all the dodgy taxis with their chatty drivers, and in uniform her beauty will make a striking contrast to those yellow heaps of junk. She has beautiful hands. The first time Raúl saw her carve up one of the hens they raise around here, big as an ostrich, he was astonished that such beautiful hands could be strong and skillful enough for the task. "As a teenager back on the ranch, I was responsible for cooking for the workers," she said. "I can feed ten or fifteen ranch hands, easy." Those hens' thighs barely fit in the bowl. You have to move them to a separate plate if you want to pick it up to sip the broth.

Aleja

Aleja brought Katerina two tennis balls to tie to her back with a strip of cloth. She read on Google that it keeps you from sleeping faceup and cranking the motor pump into gear. Aleja was tying the sash around the girl when her cell phone rang in the living room. Humberto left her a message—so lovely. God, what to do about him? He'll call again later, no doubt, pushing, insistent, eager to gobble her up like a peach in syrup. Little Red Riding Hood. Pinning her splayed against a wall, like he tried to the other day, when he'd already unhooked her bra and almost removed what she was wearing down below. Except her stockings, which are such a bear to deal with. Inhale. Ahhhh. Exhale. Serenity. Always maintaining control, knowing when to stop when appropriate. A cup of tea helps. Another deep breath. She'll need to wear jeans when she's with him—skirts are dangerous, especially that mini of hers. Aleja is one of the few women her age who can get away with wearing a miniskirt. Katerina sleeps in flannel Mickey Mouse pajamas, like a child. She's a baby. Bleary and half-asleep, she didn't understand what Aleja was asking her to do with the tennis balls. She ended up looking like she had a second pair of breasts on her back, but at least she isn't snoring. Maybe isn't sleeping either? Aleja hopes not.

Phone.

Made her jump—and that's even though she was expecting it to ring. It's him, of course. Pick up? Don't pick up? She doesn't pick up. Just what she figured: he was going to call. Almost midnight. What to do? Most likely he pays the interest but gives her the runaround on getting the principal back. Of course that's where things would end up! And at the rate the two of them are going! Yogis maintain a certain level of detachment from money, and, paradoxically, that helps them manage it and even acquire more of it, but without being greedy. The idea of the chain of yoga academies, for example, came along right when it needed to and has been developing all on its own. Each of them contributes what they have to contribute, and ultimately no one person ever deserves all the credit. Not even if Humberto had invented the concept of scaling a business! Aleja would rather maintain her personal relationship with him without having money and business stuff mixed in. She wants to hang on to Diana too, but those two are like oil and water. Better that way. She already gave him the thirty million. That's plenty. That money isn't disappearing, but it could get complicated for a while. Aleja knows that if she does everything right, she'll come out on top in the end. Treading carefully, though, because if she doesn't watch out, with those honey-colored eyes and his business savvy, Humberto will whirl her around three times and leave her worse off than when she started! And those strong, tattooed arms of his . . .

Raúl

There's nothing you can do about the salt in the saltcellars. Even regular saltshakers don't work, let alone one made with holes in a little corozo-nut spoon. On Raúl's grandmother's ranch, in another part of the coffee region, there were these little glass hens where you removed the lid and grabbed a pinch of salt with your fingers. There are three types of coffee-growing areas: humid, very humid, and extremely humid, like this one. When the fog is really soupy and hangs around a long time, Raúl lights the fireplace to combat a deeper gloom.

Nothing more beautiful than an old coffee grove, like this one here, socked in by fog. The guamas are full of parasites, and as you go through the coffee grove you suddenly run across a twisty orange tree full of moss and bromeliads of every size. On the rocks—which are very large, big as cows, as houses, as churches—are thick layers of moss with ferns growing out of them.

That was another subject Julia drove him crazy with: rocks. Every time they went out walking she would stop and stare at them with those deep black eyes of hers, and would say that rocks were living beings. If they walked past the lake, she'd say the tilapias looked like dolphins; if they walked past the rocks, they were alive. Again and again, as if expecting him to be charmed. It would infuriate anyone. And since his exasperation was obvious, Julia became surly and fights inevitably broke out.

Raúl still doesn't really understand what happened between them during the five or six months before the separation. In any case, she left him, and from there he went through some awful months. Poor Raquel had to see him at his worst, because whenever he was feeling bad he'd go to her. And what's most striking to Raúl is that even though he saw it all coming from the start, it was no use knowing it, because when it happened it was as if his flesh had been stripped from his bones. Taking off like that, leaving a note on the bedside table that started out, "I left, I'm sorry . . ." And that was it. Brutal. Deliberate—looking for revenge, to finish him off.

Raquel

Seagull tracks in the snow. They must have been up here on the roof pretty recently, since it's still snowing and the tracks haven't gotten filled in yet. Flying around at almost midnight, then. Raquel knew something like that awaited her. It's exhausting the way these things always happen to her. Nocturnal gulls now, would you look at that. Plus she heard Julia's voice clear as a bell this morning when she was coming up in the elevator with four other people. She quickly turned her head and a woman she didn't know smiled at her.

The seagulls come up from the river in front of the building, large and sturdy, fattened on fish and garbage. They follow the boats, accepting Doritos from the tourists' hands. *And you, beautiful Walt Whitman, sleep on the banks of the Hudson, with your beard toward the pole and your open hands. Soft clay or snow, your tongue is calling comrades to watch over your unbodied ghazal. Sleep: nothing's left,* says Lorca. Raquel recalls the Faulkner novel in which the boy goes around with the reader knowing he's going to commit suicide—or rather, that he's already dead. Dead souls who stick around but are no longer themselves. Living dead. Rulfo too, of course. *Your unbodied ghazal.* Gorgeous. Total García Lorca line, though Rulfo could have said it too. Julia, the living dead. It's cruel to say it, but better Julia missing than Raúl dead. You can't blame a person for their lack of talent, but you can blame them for the way they blame others for that lack. Or is everyone to blame for their own lack of talent? That could be too.

Raúl was a mess when he arrived in Inwood. His pants were falling down; not like he was skinny—that's never going to happen—but he had lost a lot of weight. And his face was wrinkled and gray, as if some slow-acting poison were sucking him dry. Raquel does sometimes feel sorry for Julia because of what happened, but the pity evaporates when she remembers Raúl's face, the bags under his eyes. She was someone who wasn't honest even with herself. A self-promoter to the end. Daggers for fingernails. Overpowering vanity. During that period Raquel was constantly reading Julia's blog, and the conceit of the woman was unbelievable. In one of her poems she was violent wind that stripped the trees on the mountain bare. Raúl must have been the mountain, Raquel figures, because of his size, and especially because of the way he stays still for so long. And the mountain was torn apart by the violent wind. To cause so much pain and then come out with such drivel! Incredible gall. And indifference. While Raúl was staggering around like a poisoned dog, she was posting poems about pigeons sunning themselves on rooftops. As if nothing were going on. And then the poem series about the murder came out, with her justifying having killed him, almost boasting. Or boasting, without the almost. She went straight from the violent wind to sunbathing pigeons to pride at having fatally stabbed her lover. Raquel remembers one line in particular: *It was imperative to kill—so I could be myself and soar.* Bloodcurdling. Now she remembers the way Julia fussed over that cat of hers and over Raúl's mutts. Julia used to say she loved animals more than she did people. She spoke to them in baby talk. People hiding behind love for animals while being hostile to people. Dangerous. For Julia, writing was everything. After murdering Raúl, she got right back to poems like the pigeon one.

She wasn't hallucinating. There are the gulls again, flying at night in the middle of a snowstorm. It's a nightmare. They're bewildered by the city's glow. She should go back down to the apartment, Raquel thinks, because this is pretty, but it isn't good, and if she stays up on the roof, who knows what kinds of things she'll end up seeing.

The tiny snowflakes falling thick look like fog.

Raúl

Raúl knew the goodbye note by heart, but he still didn't understand it:

> I left, I'm sorry. Though you judged it intellectual—and have been judging it as such this whole time—it was, in fact, my heart. My soul, my manner of being alive in this world. The way I am, all of me, entire. After your assessment yesterday, over the phone, I clearly saw what was happening to us. And now that I know more, I don't think I can be with you any longer, despite loving the place where you live, despite all the beautiful things we had together, despite losing you—a beautiful man who says he loves me and maybe sometimes does. Despite the pain I feel and the further pain to come. I have tried to figure out when it happened. And I think it

was a while ago, though I didn't know it consciously. Maybe the glass filled to the brim when I sent you the collection of poems and I couldn't understand your reaction, which was so intellectual (you this time). I got angry and went cold (remember when I called you that time and said something like, "You are breaking me apart with this"? Remember?) I didn't know the meaning of what I was saying, but I was saying something I can recognize today. And maybe the glass overflowed when I was talking to you about a writer whose work I admire and I talked about that admiration and how painfully difficult it was for me to get there, and you got angry. And now, when in response to my confessing that I don't feel you recognize me, meaning not the formal aspect of being a poet, which isn't what matters, but the heart and soul of it, your analysis and conclusion is that I'm seeking an intellectual relationship and that's not really what you're after, you're interested in a sensual relationship (I don't know if that's the word you used; if not, it was something along those lines), and you talk in veiled terms about love—and so the clarity I did not yet have came to me all of a sudden. I have poured my heart, my love, and my entire self into my writing for you and others, but you couldn't see or recognize

it. You judged it and continue to judge it as intellectual, and
so you've rejected me along with it. Thus my pain and my
rage, which you know all too well. And perhaps as a result of
that, your irritation and your silence. And your cold, ratio-
nal assessment of what I have shared with you.

Raúl is still a little wounded by it.

She left him because he didn't like her iris poems. He definitely never judged anything to be intellectual. He doesn't really
care about intellectualism or the lack of it, and he's not in the
habit of talking in veiled terms about anything. It's all pretty
tragic, when you think about it. It's as if he'd left her because she
didn't like his coconut-shell saltcellars. His saltcellars aren't him.
Raúl was in love with her flesh and her bones, her eyes, not those
poems. "This is some poorly written bullshit," Raquel said of the
note. Raúl had told Julia that he didn't like her poems much, that
what he liked was the way she looked at the world. Of course she
didn't believe him or didn't understand him. Tragic. He liked the
way she sang. Why didn't she do that instead? He liked her dark
eyes and their gaze. Nobody ever knows why they fall in love with
another person.

Raquel

Used to be, when the spirits floated in at midnight, they'd catch people sewing on their Singers, but today everybody's in front of their computers. In the ancient guts of Julia's blog, Raquel found another poem from the murder series. Premonitory. Terrifying. And a little less lifeless, artistically speaking, than her usual poems. *One day the punishment will arrive, one day the harm inflicted will reach my own body. Others will be the murderers. Others, fated to unleash the dagger, to wield death and let life go on.* So, she had to kill Raúl so she herself could take flight. A flight she never took, by the way, since, in Raquel's opinion, the stuff she wrote remained as shoddy as ever. But Julia was very aware of the harm she'd caused and knew she deserved to be punished. And even today Raúl, that big softie, is still trying to understand what happened. Like a dog trying to understand the eighteen-wheeler that's rumbling over it. Nothing to understand! What there was here was narcissism. Pathological vanity. Attempted murder. And now it would seem that death was wielded against her or some other thing worse than death, and the punishment arrived. My God!

Julián has woken up. He sounds like a horse in the bathroom when he pees. And he does splash, but less than other men Raquel has known. A few seconds from now, coming back from the bathroom, he's going to say to her, "Hey, babe," and head back to bed. Raquel's about to go lie down too, to finally rest that ever-churning mind of hers. Sometimes all she has to do is touch Julián a little and she's able to cast off the overwhelming darkness she feels. It's consolation for how exasperating, how doomed her existence is. Sex for the two of them is a blazing explosion of light, and afterward she's almost always like new again, ready to face the dreariness of this world. But not always. Sometimes the effect is the opposite; her insomnia intensifies and she goes back to the kitchen and sits in the dark with a cup of tea, with her owls and bats.

Peace always comes eventually, sometimes almost with the light of day. She sleeps two hours and then follows a hard day at school. It's difficult, when she's that sleep-deprived, to cram a bit of Joyce into the noggins of these kids from the Bronx. They liked Molly's soliloquy. And Leopold's dump after a breakfast of kidneys. *Yielding but resisting*, Joyce says of Bloom, who doesn't want the contents of his bowels to transit too quickly. Disgusting and brilliant. That fragment was a slam dunk for the kids, spurring them to read even if that's as far as it will go. Afterward they'll get a job somewhere and never pick up another book in their lives. The gringos' ignorant citizenry and violent government, and most of all their bottomless hypocrisy, Raquel thinks, have made them the world's biggest superpower. They used to give the Indians smallpox-infected blankets, and despite that they were still the good guys, the ones who gave blankets to the poor. The country with the good conscience. They're convinced that the reason they dropped two atomic bombs on a civilian population was to save lives. Quevedo and Góngora also wrote their own disgusting bits of brilliance—Joyce certainly wasn't the first. Nobody invents anything. Why bother. Inside every human being is a little boy who likes to say poop.

Julia

Aleja told me Raúl had raced around in a frenzy, staggering like a sick animal. OK, but what was I supposed to do? Early on he was calling Aleja to see if there was any chance we would get back together, but eventually he stopped doing that. He called me two or three times, but I didn't think it was appropriate to pick up. He sent a text message saying he was suffocating, to please help him, please call him. I didn't. That was the last time he tried to reach out. When I made decisions, like that one, they were complete, seamless, and I rarely changed my mind. I'd gone back to him after he wanted to split up previously because I believed we still had things to experience together. But it was different now. I was tired of our situation, and I was the one who'd decided we needed to break up. I could not be swayed. "What do you want from me, Aleja?" I asked. Please, save your opinions for matters that actually concern you.

And look now. So much peace. How deep it is!

185

Aleja

Aleja went to see if Katerina had fallen asleep. She was awake and said she was having a hard time getting used to the tennis balls. Aleja loosened the sash a little, since it was too tight around her shoulder blades. "Try again, dear," she said. "When you snore, the whole building shakes."

And there it is.

The telephone again. Don't answer, don't, Aleja thinks. If she comes across as eager, it will all fall apart. Make him realize that he's not the only beautiful one. With those legs of hers, Aleja can get any man she wants. Not touching herself there now, no. Focusing on the third eye. Inhalation empowers; exhalation purifies. With balanced breathing, we can move mountains. He hung up. He's going to call one more time and then stop bothering her for today. He won't leave a message. Ten till midnight.

How slowly the hours pass, as Daniel Santos says in that old song. After so many years of ballet, Aleja can't manage to get all that excited about tropical music. She likes certain songs, and she's a great salsa dancer, but she doesn't enjoy it as much as ballet or flamenco. In the nightclubs men always ask her if she's a professional dancer, and then, inevitably, they tell her she has a dancer's legs. Then, more inevitably still, comes the same tired proposition as always. Men are so crude. As if they expect her to respond, "I've got nice legs? Well, then yes, OK, let's go, motel, motel, motel!"

Humberto is one who knows how to do it. They'll be talking about astrology or trips through Colombia, for example, and suddenly, without knowing how or when, she's got him on top of her, bam, her all wet, him sucking her breasts. A menace. And Aleja always feels like the ghost of Julia is going to come and stare down at them from above, with Aleja letting herself get carried away and dropping all inhibitions. She's going to open her eyes with Humberto on top of her and Julia will be there all green and baggy-eyed next to the bed or the sofa, watching them with a melancholy stare. Humberto's brother, Miguel, is really handsome too, but he's arrogant. And he offered to come in as partner. The way those two have shaken her around ever since she let them get involved with her business.

Raúl

Raúl was going mad out on his ranch. So he called one of the local rattletrap taxis to take him to the airport, and he flew to Cartagena, to a seaside apartment that his friend Inés lent him. A good friend. Really worried about him. Raúl thought being at the seashore would help, but it was six days of heat and misery. He would walk along the beach like a burly ghost or a shadow at the foot of the city walls, stinking, because he kept forgetting to shower, amid the waves of tourists smelling of almond or coconut tanning lotion. Nightmarish. Hell was created in the image and likeness of the tourist cities of the tropics, and vice versa. Tourists covered in creams and wrinkles and wide-brimmed sun hats turned into demons. He would go back to the apartment at night after endless hours of walking. There were days when he walked past the same spot more than thirty times. In Parque Bolívar he smoked a million cigarettes. At night he would manage to sleep for an hour, if that, and would wake up suffocating with his soul scraped raw. Luckily the apartment was cool, ventilated by the breeze off the water. He'd go back to sleep, but without resting, as overwhelmed while sleeping as he had been while awake, and then he'd awaken again to contemplate his injuries. He was waiting for his phone to ring, keeping it always close by, though he knew Julia wasn't going to call. Raúl would look at it from time to time in case he'd gotten text messages or missed calls and hadn't heard them come in. Dawn would come and he'd go out again to walk. Again he would smoke cigarette after cigarette in Parque Bolívar. Not eating. Sometimes he would go back to the apartment in the evening and sit on the balcony, staring at the sea without seeing it. When a person manages to look at the sea and not see it, it's because they've reached their limit. Fortunately, Raúl doesn't drink. And it's a good thing he's not the suicidal type, because the apartment was on the seventh floor and would have made a nice flinging-off spot. He sent Julia a text message. She didn't answer. Raúl wished she were dead. He didn't call her again. In the depths of his suffering, he lost the little respect for her he still had. A person had to be a complete moron or totally insane to leave someone that way, over a few scribbles on a piece of paper. At the end of the day, that's all García Lorca and César Vallejo produced too: scribbles. He found it monstrous to cause another human so much suffering merely over that. She was suffocating him to death. The person who kills by suffocation dies by suffocation. The jumble of images and ideas swirled inside him, on the balcony overlooking the sea or on a bench in a plaza somewhere in the hostile historic city center, while he smoked endless cigarettes.

Odious old city.

Cartagena's poor will rise up one day and stab the tourists and toss their bodies into the sea. Unremarkable outsiders like him, sure, but especially the members of the local or international jet set you see on the streets. Enormous poverty and enormous opulence. Let's hope Inés isn't out wandering around when that happens. He should marry her someday; she is principled and intelligent and excellent company. If she isn't lynched in the uprising, of course. Recalling the delirium of sweltering grief that he experienced inside those city walls—in sunbaked plazas swarming with tourists feverish for a cheap deal alongside desperate, pushy, malnourished street vendors, descendants of the slaves who were auctioned off in those very plazas centuries earlier—Raúl appreciates even more keenly the rain he has watched so intently over the past few days that it has practically become part of him. He appreciates the darkness of the water. The mountains with their foliage, sun, and fog. This is his place. The Caribbean is beautiful, yes, but only when no one's around, only the locals. In high season it is, as Raquel says, a massive shithole. Especially if you're all fucked up, like he was.

Aleja

Whenever Aleja lets the two brothers in on her project, they really go to town. And Humberto's already been recommending another partner, a third one, but she told him no, no more, please, thanks, I'm not a businesswoman and I'd rather take things slow and not have a lot of people involved. She couldn't tell him right off the bat that she was letting him in, yes, sure, but just him. And the situation with Diana won't be easy, since she hates his guts, and if he invests, he'll want to be in charge. Aleja has to play tough or she won't get back her thirty million or make any profit. Not unless Humberto has all the capital he inherited from Julia—and a lot of it is liquid, even if he won't admit it. Julia always liked having her money accessible, a web of CDs with different maturity dates, savings accounts, that kind of thing. What Aleja needs to do is leave everything up in the air. That's the best call for now. String

Humberto along and make sure that, no matter what, he doesn't find out she owns those apartments and this building, or she'll end up in the doghouse. People think beautiful people are beautiful and nothing else. Julia herself was kind of clueless her whole life— and she was Aleja's best friend, no less. She talked down to Aleja. And since Aleja doesn't like reading much, especially not poetry, Julia assumed Aleja was dumber than she was. Aleja does read the great yoga masters so she's able to communicate their teachings in class. Yoga is born not in the head but in the heart and gut. Human emotions are so strange. Aleja doesn't understand how she could have been attached to a such a conceited creature for so long. Sometimes she wanted to kill her. Poor thing. Although she had her worthwhile qualities too.

Raúl

Unbelievable he stayed in Cartagena for so long in peak tourist season. In his agitated state, he couldn't handle the effort involved to change his flight and make his escape. Six nightmarish days, and then again airport, plane, airport. In Bogotá he went by the house for a minute to visit his siblings, then headed back to his ranch. Alberto told him he looked like he had liver disease; Lucía said hopping from place to place wasn't going to solve anything. Bus. Taxi in town. The ranch. Awful arrival. With Julia gone, everything was dead. He spent days staring at the dead bamboo, dead reeds, dead Nevado del Tolima, dead coffee fields. The days were sunny, splendorous, cool. Dead. He sent the man who was helping him out around the property at the time into town to pick up a container of energy powder, since he'd stopped eating almost entirely. He had to get out of there. If he stayed, he'd die. Raquel invited him to stay with her a few days. "I'm on my way," Raúl told her. Taxi. Airport. He willed the plane to crash and put an end to all of it.

They didn't crash. When he emerged from the Newark airport air conditioning, he was met by a wall of heat. Heat was his element in everything that happened with Julia. In August, the heat and humidity in New York were at their peak. Cartagena was cool by comparison. Strange, the sensation of being so dispirited and sweating buckets. Anguish goes better with the cold. The subway stations were fetid ovens. Human ugliness, exacerbated by his mood, was also at its peak here, as it had been in Cartagena. In both places monstrous humans pursued him wherever he went. He remembers the dodgy guy in dark sunglasses with the pink sore on his cheek. Raúl went from staggering around Cartagena to staggering around the five boroughs. Grief pursued him like the cans naughty little boys tie to cats' paws. He didn't cry in public—or in private—or scream, of course, and he even talked to anyone who struck up a conversation. He went from staring too intensely at things to staring idly into the void. He would sit for half an hour, an hour, on a bench in East River Park, or in a station way out on the F line, near the ocean, until he blearily got back on the subway and took his desolation elsewhere. He went to Sheepshead Bay many times. Name the park and he was in it. Long wanders in

Prospect Park, Central Park, Tompkins Square Park, Bryant Park, the Cloisters, and even on the far stretches of Long Island, swarming with beachgoers. Smelly, plopped on the sand, fully dressed, hours at a time, while around him people leaped around in bathing suits, tossing balls or waving rackets. One afternoon he sat down on the marble benches on the staircase that led up to the second floor of the library on 42nd Street and sobbed. That was all the weeping he did for her. People were looking at him.

To Coney Island he returned again and again, as if he were staying there and not at Raquel's apartment.

Right.

Ever since she was a little girl, Raquel has been afraid of midnight. She believes it is the hour at which death is closest.

Julia

Bad, bad Humberto! Bad Humberto!

Aleja

Katerina's tennis balls are working. She hasn't snored in ages. Success. Things tend to work out for Aleja, and that's because she's got presence. The technique of presence, proficiently performed, allows intuition to flow and, replacing the activity of the reasoning mind, dispels illusions. Katerina hasn't just stopped snoring—she's been sleeping too. She's not an ugly girl, but she doesn't seem very flexible or athletic. After two months with Aleja, though, she'll be stretchy as a rubber band and even her apnea will go away. In a year she'll have the girl ready for anything. While she's learning, keep her at minimum wage, and she could continue with her house duties too. It's an opportunity that Aleja's offering her, not a gift. They can adjust the pay later, if appropriate. Midnight. Aleja is up late again, and the problem is she doesn't feel sleepy. She needs to get her nine hours or she won't be productive tomorrow. The caffeine in the tea is what's keeping her up—it's as strong as coffee.

Phone.

She hadn't thought Humberto would call again—good sign. Maybe he'll leave a message this time, since he must have started in on the whiskey by now. Aleja doubts that Humberto has remembered Julia's birthday, and she didn't want to say anything, what for? The less they mention her, the better. Life goes on; the wheel of transmutation endlessly turns.

He's got to be drunk, leaving such an over-the-top message. He wants to kiss the blue rose of her belly, he says. Who knows where he got the crap about the rose, because he's not that poetic. All men get poetic when they're drunk. Julia used to say that when Humberto was liquored up he would get violently foul-tempered. Julia saw transgressions where they didn't exist. If she wasn't the center of attention, she'd get offended and accuse you of being foul-tempered, when she was actually the one who got furious but repressed it because she didn't like anyone to notice . . . Aleja has heard that Humberto gets difficult when he's drinking. Is that how he ended up doing what he did?

At this moment, Julia would have been turning forty-three.

Raquel

Go to bed and stop watching the snow fall, Raquel thinks. Almost twenty centimeters piled up on the fire escape, and it's still falling. They're moving away from midnight, like a piece of driftwood on the tide. The Maupassant story about the two guides who stay alone in an alpine inn during the winter and one of them goes insane. Snow can be so bleak. Here it is. Table of contents. "The Inn." Here it is. *A moving, deep and light cloud of white spray was falling on them noiselessly and was by degrees burying them under a thick, heavy coverlet of foam. That lasted four days and four nights. It was necessary to free the door and the windows, to dig out a passage and to cut steps to get over this frozen powder, which a twelve hours' frost had made as hard as the granite of the moraines.* Moraines? Don't look it up. The words you don't know are the most beautiful. Raquel's favorite word in Pombo's "Wandering Pollywog" was "orotund," when the

200

poem says, "And orotund he goes." At six, she had no idea what that marvelous word meant, and she felt no need and little desire to find out. She knew the library at home backward and forward. Raúl hung on to it—Raquel has no idea why, since he reads stuff about botany and so on, and the library was all literature. And no way was she bringing all those books to New York. They're going to rot on him down there, damp as it is. When Raquel went to visit, he told her that during the rainy season, all you have to do is dig a bit and water wells up out of the ground.

"So this isn't the rainy season, then?" she asked as the fog rolled over them, releasing fat drops of water.

"Rainy is where my mother's from," Raúl said, as if it were the logical response to Raquel's question. And he was right. In Chocó, in western Colombia, your sandals grow mold while you fan yourself in your living room.

Obviously she's not going to go to bed just to have her head keep spinning the same wheel over and over, like a hamster. She doesn't want to fuck. Julián had better not even think about it. And she's afraid of dreaming about Julia again. Raúl says that for him it's already the second time Julia has disappeared. The first was enough for him, and he'd rather not think about the second. If only Raquel liked whiskey!

Look at me, she thinks, all in a tangle over this business when I had nothing to do with it. And I'm the one who ends up with the nightmares.

Aleja

She should invite Humberto to lunch on Sunday, since Katerina
will be out. It can't be a vegetarian meal because he eats meat and
I won't measure up, Aleja thinks, heading to the kitchen to make
a cup of chamomile tea. Where did that girl put the small sauce-
pan? Everything's always moving around. And the teabags? At least
Julia's birthday is over. Even now that she's not here, she finds a
way to be a pain about it. Aleja celebrates her own too, it's not like
she denies herself that, but she doesn't make such a fuss. Where
where where did Katerina put the damn teabags? Aleja feels bad
waking the girl up just for that, so she gives up on the chamomile.
Cinnamon and clove, then. On Sunday she'll serve Humberto pork
tenderloin with prune sauce, steamed vegetables, mashed potatoes
marbled with mashed peas, red wine, crème brûlée, coffee, cognac.

The water's boiling. Men all fall in love with her and lose their heads—that's because Aleja knows how to take them to heaven, leading them by the hand, like children, down the path of sensuality. There's no reason mysticism and sensuality can't go together. And Humberto's got that gleam in his eye, unmistakable, because he saw what she is, and now he's on fire for her, hopelessly lost. And he's also aware that Aleja knows a lot about what might have gone on between him and Julia, which isn't good for him. In short, Aleja is calling the shots.

Fifteen minutes steeping so the clove and cinnamon release their essence.

Yogis have ways of knowing that the police can't even imagine. Making floating islands is easier, but Aleja prefers crème brûlée. The massive desire she rouses in Humberto is a weapon used for good, in this case, not evil. Got to borrow the mini blowtorch from Mom. And Aleja has her nine orgasms to look forward to—that was the topic of her morning class on yoga and sexuality. The book says: Nine orgasms for a woman are considered a bridge between the spiritual and physical world, since when a woman experiences them, she feels a "little death," which causes her to become one with the source of all creation, the Tao.

A little death. And that's an understatement.

Raúl

In New York Raúl endured crushing heat, going from park to park, lugging his grief along with him. A month of that, until one day he told Raquel he was going back to Colombia, and she said that yes, it was about time he got back to the ranch and back to work. Raquel thought he was doing a little better. At least he was changing his underwear now and showering.

But Raúl never made it to the ranch. In the Bogotá airport, he got the call from an architect friend who asked him if he wanted to build a chapel in a town in Caldas. The chapel would be temporary, he said, to be used only while the church was being repaired. Right there in the airport, Raúl bought a ticket and took off two hours later. He continued to stagger around. First he'd thought the sea would help, then that being in New York would help, and now the chapel in that little town.

Sonia has gone up to bed.

But this time he managed to escape from hell.

The property was beautiful and it was suitable for the task at hand. The landscape: warm coffee-growing region, fertile, spectacular. Out front were two blooming flame trees, more beautiful than any cathedral or church a human being could erect. Luckily they're still there—they didn't pull them down afterward along with the chapel. Raúl's love for the world was as huge when he saw those two flame trees as his love for God had been when he was a boy and still believed in him. His nerves were shredded, and he could have sat down to laugh or cry with joy over their bright orange flowers, but he managed to hold back. "All right, I'll build the chapel for you," he told them, and charged what his work is worth—which is to say, a lot, as usual.

He put as much energy into the project as the amount of suffering he'd experienced, but in the opposite direction, the way you stroke backward with your arms in order to swim forward. He wasn't in his normal state—far from it. He was elated. The chapel would express his intense feelings of admiration and affection for all existence. A little while back he saw the video they'd made about the project at the time, and he was surprised to find that he gave off the energy of one of those mystics who are in such a trance that they don't even have time for the occasional joke. Dilated pupils and everything. Six months of intense work and by the end of it Raúl had made it through to the other side. Sonia's arrival cemented his rescue. He hadn't forgotten Julia, of course not—still hasn't—but grief was no longer suffocating him. And even afterward, when he found out she was living with Humberto Fajardo, his reaction was not pain but surprise. Astonishment, when he found out they'd gotten married, all official, bona fide. Those two are going to kill each other, was all he thought. And ever since, a healthy indifference has slowly been gaining ground, like vegetation taking over a slope that was stripped bare.

Now he doesn't know what might happen. Nothing, Raúl figures. At this point, they're not finding her and nobody will be able to prove anything. The pain he still feels no longer has anything to do with her existing or having ceased to exist. And Raquel has only dreams. Beautiful in their horror even, but just dreams—and thank God, too, because if they were reality, this world would be as miserable as it sometimes seems to be.

Except when she dreams, Raquel is actually happy.

The fireflies are beautiful when it stops raining for a bit, like now, because the darkness of the night becomes very clean and they glow particularly bright. It's stopped raining, but there's still thunder. In less than ten minutes, the downpour is going to start up again.

Aleja

That way she can recoup her investment, get her use out of him, and enjoy herself. Tomorrow she'll wear a miniskirt. Her nine orgasms. Now she really is going to bed.

And, drifting off, she thinks, Maybe we'll even get married.

Raúl

There's so much water around these parts, there are even crabs. They look like varnished cedar wood. Fierce. When you go near them, they clack their claws with a sound like the clappers in Zen meditation. And there are snails the size of your fist, harmonious creatures, their shells the color of cedar too, with gentle curves. A craftsman could carve Raúl a snail and a crab made of wood. But there aren't too many crabs or snails either, and when Raúl comes across them, the crabs on trails with streams cutting across them, and the snails up in trees or on rocks, it's like he's seeing them for the first time.

Sonia has turned off the light.

Better turn in now, or he'll end up getting hemorrhoids.

Julia

It's true. I'm still sinking. This lake has no bottom.